# The Enemy Had It Too

# Books by Upton Sinclair

Pamela, or, Virtue Still Rewarded
Expect No Peace
Your Million Dollars
Little Steel
Our Lady
The Flivver King
No Pasaran!
The Gnomobile
Co-op: A Novel of Living Together
What God Means to Me: An
   Attempt at a Working Religion
I, Candidate for Governor
The Epic Plan for California
I, Governor of California
The Way Out: What Lies Ahead
   for America
Upton Sinclair Presents William Fox
American Outpost: Autobiography
The Wet Parade
Roman Holiday
Mental Radio
Mountain City
Boston
Money Writes!
Oil!
The Spokesman's Secretary
Letters to Judd

Mammonart
The Goslings—A Study of
   American Schools
The Goose-Step—A Study of
   American Education
The Book of Life
They Call Me Carpenter
100%—The Story of a Patriot
The Brass Check
Jimmie Higgins
King Coal
The Profits of Religion
The Cry for Justice
Damaged Goods
Sylvia's Marriage
Sylvia
Love's Pilgrimage
The Fasting Cure
Samuel, the Seeker
The Moneychangers
The Metropolis
The Millennium
The Overman
The Jungle
Manassas, A Novel of the Civil War
The Journal of Arthur Stirling

## THE LANNY BUDD NOVELS

World's End
Between Two Worlds
Dragon's Teeth
Wide Is the Gate
Presidential Agent

Dragon Harvest
A World to Win
Presidential Mission
One Clear Call
O Shepherd, Speak!

## PLAYS

Prince Hagen
The Naturewoman
The Second Story Man
The Machine
The Pot-boiler
Hell

Singing Jailbirds
Bill Porter
Oil! (Dramatization)
Depression Island
Marie Antoinette
A Giant's Strength

# The Enemy Had It Too

*A PLAY IN THREE ACTS BY*

## Upton Sinclair

Pierce Library
Eastern WITHDRAWN
1410 L Avenue
From EOU Library
La Grande, OR 97850

*NEW YORK · 1950*

## The Viking Press

COPYRIGHT 1950 BY UPTON SINCLAIR

FIRST PUBLISHED BY THE VIKING PRESS IN AUGUST 1950

PUBLISHED ON THE SAME DAY IN THE DOMINION OF CANADA

BY THE MACMILLAN COMPANY OF CANADA LIMITED

This play in its printed form is designed for the
reading public only. All dramatic rights in it are fully
protected by copyright, both in the United States
and Great Britain, and no public or private performance—professional or amateur—may be given
without formal written permission and the payment
of royalty. As the courts have also ruled that the
public reading of a play for pay or where tickets
have been sold constitutes a public performance,
no such reading may be given except under the
conditions above stated. Communications should be
addressed to the author's representative, Brandt &
Brandt, 101 Park Avenue, New York 17, N. Y.

PRINTED IN U.S.A. BY THE VAIL-BALLOU PRESS, INC.

*I would like to have this play circulated inside the Soviet Union, and I dedicate it to anyone who will make the attempt.*

*The Enemy Had It Too*

# *Characters*

IN ORDER OF APPEARANCE

DR. ROBERT ANGELL, of the Rockefeller Institute
MYRNA, his daughter
BOB, his son
ANGOBI, sub-chief of the Vichada head-hunters
GOLUBU, witch doctor of the tribe
JERRY, a guy from Brooklyn
MOTHER MARY, voice of the Lord
EBENEZER OUNCE, the most modern poet
STEVE, a tough customer
LEIF, sage from the North
ERIC, his grandson
ELFRIDA, his granddaughter
BUGSIE, a gangster
RED, his henchman
CAPTAIN ENGSTROM, of the spaceship Hastem
MORGAN, his pilot
Two ladies from Mars

## ACT ONE

SCENE:    Jungle dwelling on the Vichada River in
          eastern Colombia.

## ACT TWO

SCENE I:    Corner of Broad and Wall Streets, New York City; half-set in front. A year later.

SCENE II:    Deposit-box room in the Security National Bank on lower Broadway. The same day.

SCENE III:   Same as Scene I. The same day.

## ACT THREE

SCENE:    Before Grant's Tomb on Riverside Drive, New York. Several days later.

~~~~~~~~~~~~~~~~~~~~~~~~~~~~~~~~~~~~~~~~~~~~~

# *Act One*

SCENE: *A dwelling of the Vichada tribe on the river of that name, which rises in the Andes and flows eastward through Colombia, emptying into the Orinoco and from there through Venezuela into the Atlantic Ocean. The country is tropical jungle, and the natives are head-hunting Indians. The dwelling, ample in size, is a mere shelter, open to the audience in front. It rests upon bamboo posts with a roof of palm leaves and long grass thatch. The back and side walls are of the same materials, tied with lianas. From the roof hang various bundles and baskets made of native materials. On the floor are more baskets, also calabashes and gourds. There is a small stone fireplace at front center, with a pot over the fire. On the rear wall are pegs on which rest three blowpipes, made of reeds about nine feet long and highly polished; also quivers full of darts. There are spears with sharp tips, fishnets, and other native articles; also one rifle. There are three stools made of carved wood; three hammocks, each with a sleeping mat inside it, are hanging. A small bamboo door is at the rear. Several long red macaw feathers are stuck in the posts of the dwelling. Banana plants grow on each side. Night scene with moonlight.*

*As the curtain rises Dr. Angell is seen seated on one of the stools, stirring the pot on the fire. He is an American, about forty-five, who has been living in the jungle for fifteen years and is almost as brown as the natives. He wears a costume consisting of a loincloth made of native materials and a pair of sandals. His hair and his beard are long. From offstage comes the sound of several drums of deep tones, playing various rhythms.*

*Myrna enters; she is seventeen, slender, quiet by nature, and devoted to her father. She also is tanned by the sun. She has long blond tresses, wears loincloth and brassière, and carries a basket with fruit.*

ANGELL: So! you are here!

MYRNA: You were worried, Daddy?

ANGELL: This is a dangerous night.

MYRNA: Surely you don't have to take it so seriously. These people have been our friends for so long.

ANGELL: These people are children, my dear. Their minds are full of superstitious notions. One moment they are happy, the next they are terrified, and you can never tell which it will be.

MYRNA: You mean because Vichameni is near to death? But surely they know what old age is.

ANGELL: They do not know anything about it, Myrna. They attribute death to demons and evil spirits; and who can tell what offends these spirits or what gives them power over men?

MYRNA: You don't really believe in demons, Daddy?

ANGELL: No, dear. There are no such beings.

MYRNA: Yet you let me grow up believing in them!

ANGELL: I saw that you had to live among these people. I could not make you too different from them or they would be alien to you and suspicious of you. I wanted them to be your friends, and you to be happy here.

MYRNA: Then you do not believe that red feathers on the posts of our house keep the demons away?

ANGELL: It is a childish notion but harmless, so I let you follow the practice.

MYRNA: The white people don't have such ideas?

ANGELL: They have many just as foolish that have come down from old days. There are some who are afraid of the number thirteen, and of black cats, and of walking under a ladder, or of spilling some salt.

MYRNA: What funny ideas! You puzzle me, Daddy, for I do not know what I am to believe and what is just childish. You want people to like me, yet you will not let me marry one of the boys.

ANGELL: If you marry, you may have a child. I have always had the idea that I may take you back among the white people, and you would not want to leave your child; besides, the people here would not be willing for you to take it.

MYRNA: Yet you let Bob marry and have a child.

ANGELL: I could not refuse the offer of a head man's daughter for my son. It would have been an affront, and we could not have stayed here. Anyway, it is a different matter with a man. If he leaves, his wife and child will stay. According to Vichada custom, they both belong to the clan of the girl. They will take care of her and assign her to another husband. She will be just as happy as if she had never known a white man.

MYRNA: But you would not let Bob go head-hunting! So he is not a warrior; he is less than a man. That has given offense and interfered with friendships. Why was that?

ANGELL: It is hard to explain, dear. To go out and kill a man by stealing up on him and shooting a poisoned dart into him from a blowgun, then to cut off his head and dry it by a fire and hang it up for a trophy—that seems to white people a dreadful procedure.

MYRNA: But the white people go to war, you have told me. They have weapons far more deadly and they kill far greater numbers of people, do they not?

ANGELL: Because I belong among the white people and think them superior does not mean that I approve of everything they do. I hate war and tried my best to oppose it, but I was not able to have my way. I am a scientist—which means that I seek to understand the truths of nature, to find out how to control her ways. That we call the search for knowledge, and when we get it we give it to others, and so all the world is helped. That idea is what guides me, and if someday I take you back among the white people it will be for that reason.

MYRNA: You should tell me all about these things, Daddy. I am old enough to understand now, and I am puzzled all the time because you think the white people are superior to the Vichadas; yet I cannot see why.

ANGELL: I did not tell you, because if you thought that these people were bad, and their ways were bad, how could you play, and how could you learn to do the things that were necessary to your life? Between these Indians and the white people there is a difference of centuries, perhaps of hundreds of centuries. Your mind will grow, but theirs will not.

MYRNA, *bringing a stool and sitting down by the fire:* I think you should tell me right now, Daddy—the whole story, why we are here and why we stay. Either you like these people and their ways or you do not, and if you do not, why not leave?

ANGELL: All right, my daughter; you are seventeen, and I suppose the time has come for you to make your choice. You will wish to have a husband, and he must be either an Indian of these jungles or else a man of what we call the civilized world. I will tell you our history—a strange and terrible one. The white people built themselves great cities, they built machines which did the hard work of their world, and all of us educated and thinking people believed that the world was on its way to happiness and freedom; that the spreading of knowledge would help all mankind. But the people were divided into national groups, and these groups were suspicious and fearful of one another, and they went on building deadly weapons. A terrible war occurred, the worst in all history. When it was over, all of us thinking people agreed that this must be the last one, this must not happen again. We said it and believed it; but meantime our chiefs, the governors of the nations, went ahead building more armaments and getting ready for another war. There seemed to be no way to stop it. Each side was afraid of the other side, each said that the other was to blame, each had to prepare because the other might attack. They talked about peace while they prepared for war. So another world war came, still more dreadful. Cities were destroyed, millions of people were killed, and when it was over we all said again, "This must never happen a third time, this must be the last war"—and as before we went right on preparing for the next. We discovered new kinds of weapons and kept them secret, hoping the enemy might not know about them; but the nations spied upon one another and found out our secrets. "The enemy has it too," we said; but we acted as if we didn't really believe that. We said that the dreadful new weapons must never be used, yet we went on making them. We made bombs, a single one of which would destroy a whole city; we made what we called biological weapons—that is, germs which cause disease, and the infinitely small viruses. We would hold up some of this stuff and say that a cupful would be enough to destroy every human being on earth; we would say that this must not be used—but we went on making it and hiding it away for the rulers, the governors of the country, to use whenever they wanted to. I know that all this sounds like madness. We scientists ourselves called it that, but we went on doing it because we didn't know what else to do.

MYRNA: And then, Daddy?

ANGELL: I cannot tell you because I was not there. I was a botanist employed by the Rockefeller Institute. They asked me if I would be willing to go and live in the jungles of the Orinoco River and collect plants that might have medicinal and other uses. It seems that the doctors had discovered curare.[1] They knew that it was used by the natives to poison the darts for their blow-guns, and that it was one of the most rapid poisons known. The doctors had found that minute quantities of it were useful in certain diseases of the heart, so they wanted quantities of curare, and they wanted all the other plants that the Indian tribes of these jungles had found useful. They gave me money, and I was to use trade goods to interest the natives in collecting plants for me. So I brought my little family to Ciudad Bolívar

[1] Note: the word is pronounced koo-rah-ree, with accent on middle syllable.

on the Orinoco River and built a comfortable home. There was your mother, and you, a tiny toddler, and Bob, two years older. We lived there for nearly a year, and I was busy and happy doing what I thought was useful work. Traders now and then went up the river, taking salt and steel tools and other goods the natives wanted, and bringing back egret plumes and other things the white people wanted. I explained my wishes and made several trips with them and collected many plants and seeds.

But then came the great calamity—war. We knew about it because we had a wonderful device called the radio, by which we could hear voices from all over the world. But suddenly there was no more radio, there was only silence, and we were left to imagine what events were taking place. We waited for two or three weeks, then a small vessel came up the river to the wretched little town in which we lived. Half the men on that vessel were ill or dying. They told us they had been assailed by a terrible, mysterious disease. The nature of it no one knew, and the cure for it was beyond anyone's guessing. The men died, and then the people in the port began to die. Your mother fell ill; almost at once she knew she was doomed and said to me, "Take the children and flee. Take what you need in a dugout and go up the river. Go beyond this thing called civilization. Go and make friends with one of the native tribes, far, far beyond where the traders go." I objected that I could not leave her, but she raved at me, commanded and demanded. She was dying, I knew, and I wanted to stay and bury her, but she said, "The dead body is nothing; the mind is all that counts. Go, go! Save my children!" I obeyed her and left her dying. I put what we needed into a dugout and hired natives to paddle us up the river. We took that eight-hundred-mile journey. It took us months. We passed among enemy tribes but they let us alone, for they saw that I was a white man, and they knew that I had that terrible weapon called a gun.

Such is the story, my daughter. I picked out the Vichada River because I had heard that far up here was an old chief who had once gone down to the white men and taken back some of their goods. I found that tribe, the Vichadas, and I found that chief, Vichameni. I persuaded him to be my friend, and here we have lived. I have helped the people to the best of my ability, as you know; but now the old man is dying. His grandson is our friend, but can we count upon him in such a crisis? Golubu, the witch doctor, hates us. He has been jealous of the favors I have received from the chief, and perhaps he is really afraid that the demons are displeased by the presence of white men. Who can guess what is going on in the mind of a savage?

MYRNA: But surely, Daddy, a witch doctor will not defy the next chief.

ANGELL: A witch doctor has power over the minds of the people. What he tells them fills them with terror.

So long as things go well they are quiet, but when things go wrong, then who is to blame? Nobody can guess what these primitive minds will light upon as an explanation. Fate has willed it that the old man's illness falls upon the night of the dance of the demon god. The warriors go wild, they get drunk, they work themselves into a frenzy, and who can guess what their witch doctor will tell them about the white people and the dangers of permitting such people to live among them? You have not taken a husband; Bob has not gone out with the head-hunters, so he is not a warrior and is not permitted to attend the dance. He is not permitted to understand the drums; he is a stranger, a possible enemy, and may be displeasing to the spirits. He may bring calamities upon the tribe, not merely the death of their old chieftain, but invasion by enemies, and defeat and destruction.

*Bob enters; he is nineteen, lean and active; he wears a loincloth and is brown like his father; he has a light beard and long hair.*

BOB, *setting down the calabash he is carrying:* A present from Angobi.

ANGELL: What is the news?

BOB: Not so good. Vichameni's spirit is about to take flight.

ANGELL: And who will take his place?

BOB: His grandson; but older men will control him; and Golubu expects to control them.

ANGELL: History among the white people proves that government by priests is apt to be cruel.

BOB: Golubu is cruel, we know.

ANGELL: What are the warriors saying?

BOB: Their minds are on the dance now. They are stealing through the forest to the meeting place, hiding from the spirits who may try to stop them.

ANGELL: But a dance is never just a dance. If it has no meaning, it will acquire one.

BOB: I have talked with Angobi, and he has promised to let me know if trouble develops.

ANGELL: You really trust him?

BOB: I have hunted with him since we were children. I have saved his life and he has saved mine. He is my friend.

ANGELL: Even if others convince him that the demon god will punish our friends?

BOB: I believe he will give us warning.

ANGELL: Has he told you what the drums are saying?

BOB: They are all talking about the dance. The demon god has promised to attend.

ANGELL: That means the warriors will be in a frenzy. They will cut and slash themselves—and one another.

BOB: I would have liked to see it, Father, but I am respecting your wishes.

Pierce Library
Eastern Oregon University
1410 L Avenue
La Grande, OR 97850

MYRNA: Have you seen your wife?

BOB: She is with the other women. They hide from all men on this night. Keep yourself out of the way, Myrna.

MYRNA: They all know where we are.

BOB: There's no use giving way to fear. None of us is going to live forever.

ANGELL: No, but let us live as long as we can.

*A distant sound of many voices, women wailing; the sounds rise, and the three sit motionless.*

ANGELL: There it is. The chief is dead. All hell may break loose. They will ask the demon god to tell them who caused the chief's death; and Golubu will be the one to give the answer. I am afraid that if we do not leave here tonight we may never leave alive.

BOB: Where shall we go?

ANGELL: Down the river, to the land of the white people.

BOB: You think we three can make an eight-hundred-mile trip alone?

ANGELL: We are no strangers to jungle life.

BOB: But the rapids! The portages! We three could not carry the dugout.

ANGELL: We shall have to clear a path and cut rollers. It is downhill all the way. The task may take us a couple of months, but we can do it. This is the only season in which we would stand a chance. When the rains come the land will be flooded and the game will be driven back to the hills; we should starve. In the dry season the rocks in the river would tear the dugout or upset it.

Bob: What shall we find when we get to the white man's country? Suppose the people have all died?

Angell: We shall have to go on to other places.

Bob: Whatever it was that killed them—might it not kill us?

Angell: The virus would not last forever—it would probably be destroyed by the sun's rays. The winds would disperse it, and the rains would wash it away. I can hardly believe that after fourteen years it would be deadly in the open. We may have to be careful about going into houses.

Bob: Suppose we found no white people—should we be any better off?

Angell: We may find a boat that is seaworthy; or we can build one—a boy who was brought up on the coast of Maine, as I was, knows something about boatbuilding. It would be my idea to get to New York City.

Bob: You can build a boat to sail on the ocean?

Angell: The mouths of the Orinoco are only thirty miles from the island of Trinidad; and if we get there, I can cable to the Rockefeller Institute for funds.

BOB: But suppose there's nobody at Trinidad?

ANGELL: Geography favors us. There is a chain of islands all the way to the tip of Florida: first the Windward Islands, then the Leewards, and so on to Puerto Rico, Haiti, Cuba, and the Bahamas. There are only one or two places on that twenty-five-hundred-mile trip where we have to travel more than fifty miles from land to land. We shall be in no hurry; we can wait until the wind is fair and the weather promising. We know how to hunt and fish, and we shall not starve. It may take a year or two, but with good judgment we can manage it. Someday we may find that we can step into an airplane and be in New York in a few hours. We would find ourselves famous—the long-lost botanist and his babies, reared among the head-hunters of the Orinoco jungles. Newspaper reporters would come swarming to hear our story.

BOB: I should think, if they were so much interested, they might have sent somebody up here to find us.

ANGELL: Well, the Orinoco has scores of tributaries—it drains perhaps half a million square miles, and finding us would have been quite a task.

MYRNA: Mightn't the drums have told, if they had been asked?

ANGELL: The whole thing is a fourteen-year mystery, and we shall just have to go and find the answer. As I said, I want to live as long as I can, and I want you and Myrna to live longer.

*The drums rise again and the three sit listening.*

ANGELL: The drums sound angry.

ANGOBI, *off right:* Ahi! Hobi!

BOB: Here is Angobi! *He calls:* Hobi!

*Angobi enters; he is a painted young savage, wearing loincloth, necklaces and bracelets of jaguar's teeth, and feather headdress; his body is painted with designs, white, black, red, and ocher. The conversation is entirely in native language, but by vigorous pantomime Angobi makes clear that he is talking about Golubu the witch doctor and that Golubu is full of hate and is dancing a dance against the three whites. The words of both Angobi and Bob are accompanied by vigorous actions that give hints of their meaning.*

ANGOBI: Bo gu baligi!

BOB: Kini?

ANGOBI: Golubu! Golubu! *He imitates drum beating.* Nogo vu kanuta! O-hee huno!

BOB: Dagula ka?

ANGOBI: Golubu neeto! Hoo-ya! *He points off left.* Hoo-ya! Manu vidi bu! Mavunu lay-geh! *He points to one after another of the three.* Ta! Ta! Ta! Golubu ni-kuna!

BOB: Poli va!

ANGOBI, *making a gesture of grief:* Panivi!

Bob, *shaking his head in sorrow:* Panivi mu!

Angobi, *with alarm:* Vi-gee! Vi-gee! *He points left.*

Bob: Kani pomah!

*Bob and Angobi embrace.*

Angobi, *backing off right:* Kani pomah!

Bob: Well, there you see! He is a true friend.

Myrna: He is quite an actor. You might have thought it was Golubu crying his hate.

Angell: Well, son? The dread witch doctor declares war on us. What do you say now?

Bob: I could kill the fellow with one dart from my blowgun.

Angell: He could do the same to you, and no doubt has thought of it. You are the one who is exposed.

Bob: I could hide.

Angell: And so could we; but for how long? People cannot survive alone in the jungle.

Bob: I have other friends here, I feel sure.

Angell: And do you want to lead an insurrection in the tribe? Do you want to become its chief?

Bob: I'm trying to think it out. If I go, what shall I do about my wife and baby?

Angell: It is a hard decision, Bob. There is nothing you

can do but leave them. They belong to their clan, not to you. If you tried to take them the warriors would follow us and doubtless kill us all.

BOB: I cannot deny that.

ANGELL: And even if we could get away, what would become of her? How would she make out, a wild jungle girl in the midst of civilization? What could it mean to her? She would pine away. She is not like a white person, an individual, who can learn and change. She is a part of a clan; it would be like cutting off a finger and expecting it to survive. Soon she will be glad that you are gone, because you are different, and in her heart she must be afraid of you.

BOB: That is all true, I have no doubt.

ANGELL: More than that, my son; Myrna and I could not get out alive without you. So you will be deciding for us as well as for yourself.

BOB: There can be only one answer to that. If you have to go, I go with you.

*The drums surge loudly.*

MYRNA, *going to look off right, speaks in alarm:* Golubu is coming!

ANGELL: So he will tell us himself! *To Bob, who leaps and seizes the rifle:* Don't shoot him!

BOB: Not unless he insists on it. *He darts out of door at center, leaving it partly open and standing behind it.*

GOLUBU, *calling off right:* Ho wangoni! Ho zoba!

*He enters, dancing and prancing, in a state of frenzy; the tribal medicine man, in fierce get-up, is naked except for loincloth and necklaces and girdle chains of huge crocodile teeth. He is painted all over with serpents; he carries a rattle and has bark boxes dangling from his waist; his headdress is of brilliant macaw feathers. He has come to intimidate the whites and drive them away; his features and gestures are full of menace. He makes faces at them, invokes the demon god against them; stamps his feet, slaps his thighs, points offstage left, where the river is supposed to be. He dances in front of Angell, then in front of Myrna, both stare at him but do not speak; his dancing is a sort of half-crouched prancing; it is supposed to constitute a spell upon them. He leaps about the room, waving his hands at this and that, putting a spell upon everything.*

GOLUBU, *pointing toward the river:* Hoo-ya! Hoo-ya! Manu vidi bu! *He prances to the posts, on which Myrna has fastened long red macaw feathers; he tears each one down and stamps on it.* Manini ga! ga! Valughi! *He prances out, then turns, flinging his arms in a wild gesture, and points left again.* Hoo-ya! Hoo-ya! *He dances off right; the drums die down.*

ANGELL: Well, there is no misunderstanding that!

BOB, *re-entering through door, with rifle:* He has torn down our feather guards and left us exposed to the evil spirits.

MYRNA: Daddy says there are no evil spirits.

BOB: I'd hate to take a chance on it this night.

ANGELL: When Golubu has pronounced a spell he is bound to make it good. *He* will be the evil spirit.

BOB: He has given us fair warning. Do you wish to go?

ANGELL: I can see no choice.

BOB: If we're going it should be quickly, while the warriors are busy with the dance.

ANGELL: Do you wish to see your wife?

BOB: I would not be allowed to see her on the night of the demon god. And, anyhow, what could I say?

ANGELL: You might cause interference with us.

BOB: If we are going we have but one thing to do—stow our things in the dugout and start. We made it ourselves, so no one can call it theft.

ANGELL: It will be a hard trip—and a wet one.

BOB: We know the river.

MYRNA: Surely we cannot run the rapids at night!

ANGELL: We shall have to tie up to an overhanging branch and wait for daylight.

MYRNA: But the crocodiles, Daddy!

ANGELL: There are crocodiles and caymans, there are

caribe fish and pythons and jaguars—but nowhere are there any creatures so dangerous as men. What the animals will do can be foreseen, but no one can foresee what may come into the mind of a man.

MYRNA: Will the hostile tribes attack us?

ANGELL: Perhaps not, if we go quickly and do no harm to them. They know what a rifle is, and they have no means of knowing that we have only three cartridges left.

BOB: They may take it to mean that trade is coming back to the river and that they will be able to get salt again.

ANGELL: The nearer we get to the white man's world, the more apt they will be to think that.

BOB: Let us get to work. We must travel light, remembering the portages. Shall you try to take your specimens?

ANGELL: It would break my heart to throw away fourteen years of collecting.

BOB: All right, we'll try to get them through.

ANGELL: The seeds are the most important. We may find that we ourselves are seeds.

BOB: We will try to get ourselves and the other seeds through in safety. *He piles two of the wicker baskets and carries them off left.*

MYRNA: Shall we take our cloaks, Daddy?

ANGELL: We are going to a cold country, colder than you can imagine. Water becomes hard as rocks.

MYRNA: How can we paddle in it then?

ANGELL: This does not happen to the ocean, but to lakes and the smaller streams. We shall have to find more clothing, or learn to make it.

MYRNA: I was so proud when I learned to weave cloth out of grasses. *Out of a wicker box she lifts three grass cloaks, folds them carefully, and packs them into a flat basket.* How strange it seems to be leaving the only home I have ever known!

ANGELL: We will find a better one somewhere—or make it. You will see many strange things and be kept busy learning about them.

MYRNA: And will you be finding me a husband, Daddy?

ANGELL: In the white man's world the girls are not in such a hurry to find husbands. You are still very young in their eyes. *As they talk they are assembling their belongings.*

MYRNA: It is fortunate that we dried so much tapir meat.

ANGELL: Indeed yes, for we want to spend the daylight hours traveling. But we can catch fish as we go.

MYRNA: Shall we take this fruit?

ANGELL: We have plenty of room in the dugout. When we come to a long portage we may have to throw the heavy things away.

MYRNA, *starting to take bundles that hang from the ceiling:* I am terribly excited, Daddy. It is my first long trip.

ANGELL: When the river is swift it is dangerous; and when it becomes larger and slow, we shall have to paddle in the burning sun. Life in the jungle is always hard.

MYRNA: Yet you say there are no evil spirits! Who made it that way?

ANGELL: That is what the world calls philosophy. If I knew the answers, I should be the wisest of all white men. We can talk about such problems on the way. Now we have to be sure to forget nothing we may need.

MYRNA: I suppose we take all our weapons?

ANGELL: We shall depend mostly on the blowguns. Small game is what we shall live on.

MYRNA: Have you thought, Daddy, that this dreadful thing you call "virus" may have killed the game?

ANGELL: I have thought about it often. From what the laboratory men used to tell me, there are some viruses that affect humans and not animals; there are other viruses that affect some animals and not others. It is impossible to know what we shall find.

MYRNA: What an adventure for a girl!

ANGELL: All life is an adventure, my daughter; and that is the way to take it.

BOB, *entering left:* Well, everything is all right.

ANGELL: I was afraid someone might have damaged the dugout.

BOB: It seems to be sound. I won't put the things in until we get it into the water.

ANGELL: The Vichadas are not thieves. I would much rather trust a head-hunter than some people I have known in the civilized world.

BOB: I will pack the load so that we have a level place to lay the blowguns. They are the most precious things we shall carry, and they must not be warped.

MYRNA: Have we enough curare?

ANGELL: I'm afraid not; and it is one thing we cannot get or make on the way.

BOB: I spoke to Angobi, and he promised to bring us a supply. I may have to go and find him.

ANGELL: Let us lay out the loads. *He begins enumerating the articles while laying them in three piles on the floor.* Paddles, spears, rifle, quivers, fishnet, fishing tackle—

BOB, *standing on stool and taking down bundles:* Dried tapir meat, dried anaconda meat, manioc meal.

MYRNA: Do we take our hammocks?

ANGELL: As far as we can; but when we come to rapids that are miles long, we may wish to reduce the weights we carry on our backs.

MYRNA: Oh, my lovely hammock with the black squirrel tails!

BOB: What we have to think about is to keep the dugout from upsetting and giving everything we have to the river spirits.

MYRNA: Are there river spirits, Daddy?

ANGELL: There are river rapids and river rocks. There are crocodiles, and razor-toothed caribe fish that tear the flesh from your bones in half a minute. That is enough.

BOB: Let's keep our minds on this job.

ANGOBI, *calling off right:* Ahi! Hobi!

MYRNA: There is Angobi.

BOB: Hobi!

ANGOBI, *carrying earthen pot, about the size of a half-pint, carefully sealed on top:* Curare. Curare noto.

BOB, *taking the pot:* Zumo. Inano zumo.

ANGELL: Poliva.

ANGOBI: Panivi! *He makes signs of sorrow.*

BOB: Panivi mu. *To Angell:* May I give him part of our salt?

ANGELL: Surely.

BOB, *taking a small package from one of the bundles and handing it to Angobi:* Ah-ghee.

ANGOBI, *with excitement:* Inano zumo. *With sadness:* Kani pomah. *He clasps Bob's hand and holds it.*

BOB: Kani pomah.

*Angobi goes to Angell and repeats the ceremony, then backs away, repeating the words of parting. Myrna, a woman, does not count and remains silent. Angobi exits right.*

BOB: It is a good thing to know that a savage can be a true and honest man.

ANGELL: We can only hope that we may find some as good in the world of the white men. God help us! Well, we must be going. Put that jar of curare in the basket with the seeds. If we should have an upset, that will keep it afloat and we can perhaps save it.

BOB: All right. *He proceeds to pack as directed.*

ANGELL: Myrna, you will carry the blowpipes. Keep them safe at all hazards. They will float, of course. They

are most important to us, far more important than the
rifle. Guard the quivers of darts also. *She takes them.*
I will carry the basket of robes.

BOB, *pointing to the pile:* I can manage these bundles.

ANGELL: I guess I can take the rest. *He looks around.*
Can you think of anything we are forgetting?

BOB: We have them all.

*They stand looking around.*

ANGELL: We are parting with fourteen years of our
lives. It seems to call for a ceremony. I remember a
noble poem by an English poet named Tennyson. He
was speaking the words of an old-time Greek. *He recites:*

> Come, my friends,
> 'Tis not too late to seek a newer world.
> Push off, and sitting well in order smite
> The sounding furrows; for my purpose holds
> To sail beyond the sunset, and the baths
> Of all the western stars, until I die.

BOB: Well, let us hope that we do not die until we have
seen the wonderful white world. Off we go.

*He loads up his burdens and exits. Angell follows.*

MYRNA, *looking around her:* Good-by, little house! The
only house I've ever lived in! *She hesitates, then picks
up one of the red feathers lying on the floor and sticks it*

*into her hair, smiling to herself.* Perhaps there are no river spirits, but anyhow it will be pretty to wear a red feather. *She exits.*

**CURTAIN**

~~~~~~~~~~~~~~~~~~~~~~~~~~~~~~~~~~~~~~~~~~~~~~~~

# *Act Two*

SCENE I: *Half-set in front of stage. The stage is supposed to be at the foot of the steps of the Sub-Treasury Building. The backdrop shows a view of Wall Street with the House of Morgan on the corner at the right, and the Stock Exchange across the street to the left; other financial buildings are beyond. There are automobiles in the view but no human beings.*

*As the curtain rises the stage is bare. After a pause long enough for the audience to take in the scene, Angell, Myrna, and Bob stroll on at left and gaze around them with curiosity. They are dressed as in Act I; each carries a straight, highly polished blowgun, with a small quiver of darts hung over the shoulder. These darts are thin, not more than a quarter of an inch; each is about fourteen inches long, with needle-sharp point, and the base is wrapped with tree cotton so that it fits precisely into the blowgun. A puff of breath from the cheeks shoots it out with great force. Neither end of the blowgun is ever allowed to touch the ground.*

*When the three reach the center of the stage they stop and face the audience.*

ANGELL: This is an interesting spot. It was the financial

center of America, and indeed of the world. *He points high toward the audience:* This building is the United States Sub-Treasury, where the money of the government was kept; this one—*he turns and points*—as you see from the sign, was J. P. Morgan and Company. It was the headquarters of the firm that had more influence upon financial affairs than the government itself. At least that was true when I was a child, and long before that. This is Wall Street that you are looking down, and here was the Stock Exchange, where all the trading in stocks and bonds was done. The House of Morgan was always a storm center of controversy. The old man who founded it was a sort of king.

MYRNA: He was so very rich?

ANGELL: It was rather that the very rich people trusted him, and he became the boss by their general consent.

MYRNA: Like Vichameni.

ANGELL: Just so. Every now and then there would come a panic, and old J. P. Morgan would take charge, and everybody would obey him and think that he had saved them. The Reds hated him bitterly; one time there was an attempt to blow up this building with a bomb. It was loaded upon a rickety old wagon drawn by a white horse. It came while this street was crowded with people, and in front of the building the bomb went off. It killed and maimed great numbers of people, but it didn't hurt the House of Morgan, and it didn't stop the operations of the Stock Exchange.

MYRNA: It must be strange to you to see this place all silent and deserted.

ANGELL: I can hardly believe that this is the corner of Broad and Wall Streets and that I am here, alive and not dreaming.

BOB: The strangest thing, it seems to me, is that there are no skeletons lying about.

ANGELL: The plague must have struck gradually. When people died they would be carried away; or at least they would crawl indoors.

MYRNA: Or perhaps run away to the country?

ANGELL: They would have come back after a time. The plague could hardly last forever. The sun would shine and perhaps kill the virus, and the rains would wash it away, or at any rate diminish its intensity.

BOB: You have no idea what this virus was?

ANGELL: A virus is an extremely small object, so small that it has to be magnified one or two hundred thousand times so that you see it. The viruses are living things, and they multiply after the fashion of all creatures, so the tiniest quantity would suffice, and if you got it you would be dead in a few hours. The scientists didn't deal with the problem of how these substances were to be distributed; they left that to the military men. It could be scattered into the air; it could be put into the water that people drank or into the food they ate.

MYRNA: How could it happen that your scientific men would work at such dreadful things?

ANGELL: Their consciences troubled them, and I have heard them talk about it. They would say, "Whatever we get, the enemy will get it soon." Presently they would be saying, "The enemy has it too." I have heard them say, "This thing is so dreadful that whichever side uses it first will exterminate the other side." They would go back and talk about what happened during the Second World War, when both sides had poison gas, but these gases were so terrible that neither side dared use them, knowing the other side would use them also. But when you get what they call an absolute weapon, something so terrible that it wipes your enemy out, that motive no longer operates. The only thing left was the hope that the enemy's moral sense wouldn't permit him to use it. But apparently the enemy didn't have the same kind of moral sense that we had; and so it seems that New York City no longer has any inhabitants.

BOB: We will have to make a search.

ANGELL: As a matter of precaution, let's agree that if anything should happen to separate us, this is our meeting place—the steps of the Sub-Treasury Building at the corner of Broad and Wall Streets. We must agree that we will not enter any building, at least not until we have consulted and decided that it is a necessary risk.

Bob: All right, it's understood.

Myrna, *pointing off right in excitement:* There's a man!

Angell: Sure enough; and he sees us. Now remember, we have to be careful. He may be a friend or he may be an enemy; there is no way to tell.

Bob: And he may have the virus.

Angell: There's no way to tell about that. We have to keep our distance.

Bob: And keep darts in our blowguns.

Angell: Of course. We have an advantage there because people in New York think of a blowgun as a child's toy. He sees us and is coming, so evidently he is not afraid. *He calls:* Hello, stranger!

Jerry, *off right:* Hello yourself! What sort of people are you?

Angell: We are Americans. We have been living in the jungles of South America.

Jerry: Have you got the Bio down there?

Angell: What do you mean by the Bio?

Jerry: I mean what kills people.

Angell: We haven't got it so far as we know, but we'll keep our distance and you keep yours.

Jerry: You bet there don't nobody get near me. *He en-*

*ters and stands about fifteen feet away. He is a guy
from Brooklyn, in his thirties, dressed in ordinary street
clothes, which are worn, dingy, and shapeless. He is
anxious but at the same time curious.* How long you
been here?

ANGELL: We just landed.

JERRY: From what?

ANGELL: From a small sailboat we found and repaired.

JERRY: Must have took you a long time to come in a
sailboat from South America.

ANGELL: It took us over a year.

JERRY: Did you see any people on the way?

ANGELL: We saw a few here and there, but they were
afraid of us and kept out of our way.

JERRY: That's the best way to live. If you get near the
Bio, that's your finish.

ANGELL: We were fourteen years in South America, so
we don't know much about it. I suppose by Bio you
mean biological weapons, or something of the sort.

JERRY: When there was newspapers I used to read long
words like that. Now there ain't no newspapers, so I forget them.

ANGELL: How did you manage to escape the Bio?

JERRY: Lucky, I guess; anyhow, I'm alive.

ANGELL: How do you live?

JERRY: I found a place where there's canned food, and no poison. I stay there and I don't go into no other houses.

ANGELL: Are there other people here?

JERRY: You see one now and then, and you get to know them, but you keep to windward of them if you can.

ANGELL: Not very much fun, I would think.

JERRY: Nobody thinks about fun any more, they just think about keepin' alive. What was you, mister?

ANGELL: I was a botanist, sent to the jungles of South America to find plants that might be of use to the doctors.

JERRY: No doctors no more—at least I ain't come on one. There's drugstores, but I dassn't go in 'em. These young people your family?

ANGELL: This is my son Bob and my daughter Myrna.

JERRY: My name's Jerry. I'm a guy from Brooklyn, but I ain't been there for years. What's the use? You find a place where you got some food and there ain't no Bio. How come you folks come here?

ANGELL: Well, New York had been my home and I wanted to see what had happened here. Would you mind telling me about it?

JERRY: Sure, I'll tell what I know. Mind if I sit down?

ANGELL: Not at all. We'll sit too.

*All of them sit on the sidewalk where they are, Jerry about fifteen feet away.*

JERRY: This seems to be a safe distance. It ain't good manners to come nearer.

ANGELL: Thank you for telling us.

JERRY: I'll tell what I know, but it ain't much. All of a sudden people began to die wholesale; they died in their beds, they died on the streets. At first they buried them, but then there wasn't enough left to bury them. Everybody ran away into the country, but it didn't do much good because the farm people thought it was the city people that had got the poison and they took to using shotguns to keep us away. You couldn't know where to go because there wasn't no newspapers, and no way to find out; the radio quit, there wasn't no electricity, and there wasn't no lights, and there wasn't no water. You had to go up to the reservoy to get water. Everybody said it was the Bio, and the enemy had done it. They said we must do it to the enemy too. Maybe we did, I don't know. It was all war secrets and they didn't tell us. I went to the country for a while but I couldn't get no food. I stole some, but it was too dangerous; people was getting shot all the time, so I decided to come back to the city. There wasn't hardly anybody here by then. I got water from the reservoy and got canned food and I slept outdoors and stayed alive. And then there come the rats.

ANGELL: The Bio didn't kill the rats?

JERRY: There come to be swarms of them. I suppose they et the dead bodies, but we dassn't go into the houses to see. Pretty soon there was so many they hunted in packs. You dassn't go out of your hiding place at night and you kep' the door shut tight. I suppose there were no more bodies, so they et each other. Now you don't see them no more, so I suppose they et everything. Maybe they went out into the country. Do you suppose they could swim the rivers?

ANGELL: They might. Anyway, they could go by the bridges and the tubes.

JERRY: It's awful what's happened to the world. Do you suppose it's happened to the rest of the country?

ANGELL: If it hadn't, people would have come here by now.

JERRY: If you go into houses, pretty soon you don't come out; so if you want to live you stay in the place you know. You folks figuring to stay in the city?

ANGELL: We have no plans.

JERRY: I might be willing to share my secrets with you. I'd like to be friends with this young lady.

ANGELL: Did the Bio get the women more than the men?

JERRY: It seems like. All I know is that you don't see many women.

ANGELL: It was just the opposite in the jungle where we came from. The men killed each other off by head-hunting, and so many men could have extra wives.

JERRY: There is men in this town who would go to that place if they knew about it. *He turns to Myrna.* Would you be willing to keep company with me, miss?

MYRNA: I might. We could talk it over.

JERRY: I've got a very good place, and it's hard to find one. I never told nobody else, but I will tell you folks. I got a warehouse full of canned goods and there is wine and liquor, and there is mineral water. I watch every time I go in to make sure I'm not bein' followed. I watch every time I go out to be sure there's nobody near me.

ANGELL: You are indeed a friend worth having. We'll consider the matter.

JERRY: Oh, Doc, it's a lonesome world now! It's awful to look back and think what good times we had.

ANGELL: What did you do, Jerry?

JERRY: I was a batboy for the Dodgers. And, oh, I never knew how lucky I was! It was like bein' in heaven—all them wonderful games—and now it's all gone and there'll never be another Woild Series!

ANGELL: Hard lines, Jerry!

MYRNA, *looking off right:* There's a woman.

BOB: Sure enough! A black one.

JERRY: That's Mother Mary, she's called. She'll save your soul if you'll let her.

MYRNA: Save my soul?

JERRY: She was a preacher but she ain't got many to work on now. *He calls:* Hello, Mary!

MARY, *off left:* What sort of folks is them?

JERRY: They're all right folks; they won't hurt you.

MARY: What sort of folks are they—goin' half naked? Don't they know that nakedness is sin?

MYRNA: It was all right where we came from, Mary; you don't need to be afraid of us.

MARY: I ain't taking no chances. Keep your distance. *She comes on and stands some distance away; she is a large, stout Negro woman dressed in a long Mother Hubbard wrapper, very much worn. She walks with a cane.* What's them long things you got?

ANGELL: Those are music pipes.

MARY: They make pretty music?

ANGELL: Very pretty indeed.

MARY: I would like to hear that music. I have not heard

any for years and years—only what I make myself.

ANGELL: Someday you shall hear it.

MARY: What part of the country you folks from?

ANGELL: From South America.

MARY: I come from the South too—South Carolina. But what sort of folks is you? It's a sin in the sight of the Lord for a girl to be seen half naked with men standin' by and starin' at her. The Lord has sent me to preach righteousness.

MYRNA: Where I came from, Mary, we had no other clothes.

MARY: I got an extra dress that I'll give you fo' the sake of our heavenly Father. O Lord, save the sinners!

ANGELL: You are an evangelist, Mary?

MARY: I'm an aposteless of the Lord. Before He rebuked the wickedness of this city I preached to thousands and brought them to the mercy seat. I wore a white silk robe and a white silk cap. I had ten white-robed angels, and a choir with a hundred voices, and the altar was hung with the crutches of them that was healed. They was saved, every one, by an immaculate miraculous miracle. We sang—oh, glory, how we sang!

*She sings:*

> Why don't you pray for me sometimes?
> Why don't you pray for me sometimes?

> You pray for me and I'll pray for you,
>
> Oh, why don't you pray for me sometimes?

That was the way I sang, and when I preached I punched the devil in the eye, I did. Dance and sing and clap yo' hands!—yea, brethren and sistern! I lived in the finest house in Harlem, and many waited upon me out of love for what I taught them; there was no one in the place that did not heed the words of Mother Mary the aposteless. Now the Lord has took them righteous ones unto Himself, and them that heeded not His words has been cast into everlasting flames. He left me here to save the remnant. The Lord in His mercy save you and bring you to His golden throne.

ANGELL: That's fine, Mary, but first we have to find some place to live here.

MARY, *wheedling:* Would you like to have a good cook? I can make the best spoon bread—if I got the makin's.

ANGELL: If we can get them we'll let you know.

MARY: Take my advice and put clo'es on that young woman quick. There is evil men that roams these streets, and a young woman in her near nakedness is no sight to put befo' them.

MYRNA, *looking offstage left:* Here comes a man now.

ANGELL, *addressing Jerry:* Do you know this one?

JERRY: No, Doc. He's a new one. Looks queer.

ANGELL, *calling:* Hello, stranger. Who are you?

VOICE OF OUNCE, *offstage left:* I am a poet. I am the founder and creator of modern poetry.

ANGELL: Welcome, Poet; but don't come too close.

VOICE OF OUNCE, *sounding nearer:* A poet has no need of closeness; a poet lives within his own soul.

*The others wait. He enters; he is a rather small, frail man with long reddish beard and hair. He wears blue denim overalls and a faded and dingy shirt; his shoes are worn and dirty.*

ANGELL: We welcome a disciple of the Muses. We are wayfarers meeting by chance. Tell us about yourself.

OUNCE: My name is Ebenezer Ounce. I come from our national capital, riding on Shanks's mare—or, as the Chinese poet says, "*Li fuo ko.*"

ANGELL: That's a long journey, from Washington.

OUNCE: I am seeking my pupils and disciples. I have raised up a new school of poets whose boast it is that they understand only one another—or, as the Arabian commentator says, "*Hakbatak rustabak.*"

ANGELL: A truly learned scholar, I perceive. The fates have dealt harshly with you.

OUNCE: The government declared me insane and put me under lock and key, but I have survived them all; I have survived the judge and the jury, the bailiffs and the keepers and the doctors. I have survived the critics also. As the Ethiopian sage has so well expressed it, *"Bgargashu nbongo guo"*—my wisdom will survive the ending of the world.

ANGELL: It may be that you have survived your disciples, Mr. Ounce.

OUNCE: I can always make new ones wherever my voice penetrates. If you'd be interested, I should be glad to recite from one of my cantos.

ANGELL: I am sure we should be delighted, sir.

OUNCE, *recites with great solemnity:*

> On earth's shelter cometh oft to me,
> Eager and ready, the crying lone-flyer,
> Whets for the whale-path the heart irresistibly,
> O'er tracks of ocean; seeing that anyhow
> My lord deems to me this dead life
> On loan and on land, I believe not
> That any earth-weal eternal standeth
> Save there be somewhat calamitous
> That, ere a man's tide go, turn it to twain.

And what do you think of that, sir?

ANGELL: Well, it has an impressive sound, but I am obliged to confess that I do not understand it.

OUNCE: Ah, that is because you make the mistake of trying to understand poetry with your mind.

ANGELL: How does one understand poetry?

OUNCE: Only with the blood, sir! Only with the blood!

ANGELL: Unfortunately I have never learned to do that.
But perhaps some of the others— *He looks inquiringly
to the company.*

MARY, *excitedly:* I understand! I understand with the
blood! It is the blood of the Lamb! *She sings ecstati-
cally:*

Are you washed in the blood of the Lamb?
Are you going to glory? Yes I am, yes I am, yes I am.
Are you washed in the blood of the Lamb?
Are you going to glory? Yes I am.

OUNCE, *disgustedly:* Who is this woman?

MARY: I am the aposteless of the Lord, the Ancient
of Days that endureth after the world. I am your sister
in the blood.

OUNCE, *to the others:* I'm not interested in this crazy
creature.

MARY, *in fury:* You call me crazy, man? You that just
broke out of an asylum?

OUNCE: I did not break out; the asylum came to an end.

MARY: I know what you is. You is one of them Reds.

OUNCE: Oh, ho, ho! The government would be interested to hear that! They accused me of being a Fascist because I made speeches for Mussolini.

MARY: All the same, you is a Red.

OUNCE: What makes you say it?

MARY: Look at that beard o' yourn.

OUNCE: I can't help the color of my beard any more than you can help the color of your skin. If I am a red Communist, you are a black Fascist.

MARY, *striding toward him:* Don't you call me no names, you limb of Satan! *As she lifts her cane he backs away.* I'll send you to the place where you belongs! *She starts to run at him; he turns and flees off left and she follows.*

ANGELL, *laughing with the others:* It seems that only the queer people are left in this great city.

JERRY: You get queer when you stay by yourself all the time. You ought to know that, Doc.

ANGELL: I suppose that's true; and yet you are not so queer.

JERRY: You ought to see me alone, Doc. Sometimes I ketch myself cryin' when I think there ain't a-goin' to be no Woild Series this year.

MYRNA: What is a Woild Series?

JERRY: It was baseball games, miss, that come at the end

of the season for the championship. Dem Bums and the
Yankees usually fought it out, and forty thousand people come and yelled their heads off, and all over the
country millions of people was listening to the radio
or watchin' television, and couldn't do nothin' else. Oh,
miss, it was the most wonderful thing ever, and I was
right in the middle of it every year. If you had been
there I could of got you a ticket, and I would of took
you.

ANGELL, *smiling:* It is not the least of our losses.

MYRNA, *looking off left:* Here comes another man.

JERRY: He's no good. Keep out of his way.

ANGELL: He has seen us, and we cannot avoid him.

JERRY: His name's Steve, and he's a tough customer.
He's got it in for me, so I'm gone. *He exits right in a
hurry.*

BOB: Spread out a little.

*He takes a position downstage, his father upstage, and
Myrna between them. All three of them stand watching.
Steve enters; he is in his twenties; he has a hard face
and is grim in manner; he wears a pair of ragged trousers; is barefooted and has no shirt. His right hand is in
his trousers' pocket.*

STEVE: Hello.

ANGELL: How do you do?

STEVE: Where did you come from?

ANGELL: From South America, in a sailboat.

STEVE: How long you been here?

ANGELL: Just a couple of hours.

STEVE: This girl. What's she? Your daughter?

ANGELL: Yes.

STEVE: And this fellow?

ANGELL: He's my son.

STEVE: And them pipes. What are they for?

ANGELL: Those are our music pipes.

STEVE: Music, eh? I don't like the looks of them. Put them down.

ANGELL: They are harmless, I assure you.

STEVE: All right, they won't harm me on the ground. Drop them. *He draws a gun and aims it at Angell.* Do what I say.

ANGELL: This is not very polite, my friend.

STEVE, *with a hoot:* Polite! When you've been on your own for fifteen years like me you don't worry none about politeness. Drop them things on the ground! Do what I say and do it quick!

ANGELL: And what then, my friend?

STEVE: I'll tell you then. First I tell you, drop them things. I'll count ten and I won't count slow; if you ain't done it then, one of you dies. One, two, three, four, five, six— *They lay down their blowguns.* That's better. Now I want this girl.

ANGELL: What do you want her for?

STEVE: I'll tell her that. I ain't seen a young woman for years, and I want this one. What you two guys do is to turn around and walk—and walk fast.

ANGELL: And if we don't?

STEVE: Then one of you will lie here and the other will walk alone. Now quick—go. *They stand with clenched fists and grim faces.* All right then, I'll count again: one, two, three, four, five, six, seven, eight, nine, ten. *They are still standing and he raises the automatic gun and fires at Bob.*

BOB, *putting his hand to his shoulder:* I'm shot!

STEVE: You got that one through the shoulder; the next one will be through your guts.

MYRNA, *quickly:* Hino hungo! Hino! Curare!

STEVE, *sharply:* What's that you're saying?

MYRNA: I am telling them that I like you. You are a brave man. I want them to go.

STEVE: Why couldn't you say it in English?

MYRNA: They will know better that I mean it; I want them to go. Go quickly.

STEVE: All right, what's the answer? *They hesitate for a moment longer, then turn their backs and walk slowly off right.* Keep going, and no nonsense. Remember that if either one of you turn around you die. And don't try to follow me, because I'll keep watch and I'll turn lots of corners. I'm a dead shot and I won't waste a bullet; but I got plenty in my pockets. Ask anybody in this town; they know me and they do what I tell them. *Angell and Bob walk slowly off. Steve keeps the gun trained on them for a considerable time after they are offstage. Then, without taking his eyes off them, he says to Myrna:* All right, baby, now it's your turn. I got everything you need, and if you ain't got the Bio yet you won't get it from me. Will you do as I say?

MYRNA: I will, of course.

STEVE: My name is Steve and I give the orders. I'll back away till them guys are out of sight. You come along about ten feet after me and a little bit to the right. I don't want to hit you if I have to shoot at them; it's up to you to live or die. Don't try no tricks because I'm a dead shot, and I mean every word I say. Understand that?

MYRNA: I understand.

STEVE: All right then.

*He starts to walk backward left and Myrna follows. His eyes keep turning quickly from her to the men offstage and then back to her. He backs offstage and Myrna follows. The curtain falls after they are out of sight.*

**CURTAIN**

SCENE II: *A private deposit-box room in the Security National Bank, New York. Everything in this room is of the utmost elegance; chromium, expensive polished furniture, and chairs upholstered in Moroccan leather. There is a steel-barred door at right. At left is a heavily barred window with sunlight streaming in. Along the entire upstage wall of the room are tiers of safety-deposit boxes of various sizes. To the front are a couple of tables at which the customers sat to clip their coupons and sort out their treasures. Chairs are in front of these tables. The tables are equipped with pens and ink and lamps—but there is of course no electricity. Steve has taken the place for his residence, and there are all the signs of his living therein, on a crude picnic basis: a pallet made of blankets on the floor, and more blankets to cover him; a small oil stove, many cans of food, some empty; an old overcoat hanging up; pots and pans and numerous other signs of occupancy.*

*As the curtain rises the stage is unoccupied. After sufficient time to allow the audience to take in this unusual combination of past and present, footsteps are heard coming down the staircase and Myrna emerges, followed closely by Steve with the pistol at her back.*

STEVE: Well, this is it, baby. Your new home. How do you like it?

MYRNA, *looking around bewilderedly:* I can't say, because it looks so strange.

STEVE: Nothing like it in the jungles of South America, I suppose.

MYRNA: Surely not.

STEVE: This is the Security National Bank of New York, and this room is where the rich guys had their stocks and bonds locked up. You're safe here. The rats can't get at you, and nobody else can get at you, and I'm tellin' you in advance, when I have to go away I'm goin' to lock you in, and you'll be safe from all the world—and will be here for sure when I get back.

MYRNA: That doesn't sound like a very kind way to treat a woman.

STEVE: Ha! Ha! We'll see about being kind after you get to know me better, and after I'm sure you'll behave yourself and not disappear in this big city.

MYRNA: I'd have no idea where to go in this city, and I could hardly survive without you.

STEVE: Well, that sounds like a sensible dame. You behave yourself, baby, and we'll soon be friends.

MYRNA: If you will treat me right I will be a good wife. I am long past the age when I would have been married among the Indians.

STEVE: I thought you said you was an American girl.

MYRNA: I was only two years old when I was brought to that country, and I never knew any other place or way to live.

STEVE, *making a move toward her:* Kiss me, baby.

MYRNA, *stepping back from him:* Oh, no! Wait. Please!

STEVE: Don't you know you're gonna kiss me, baby?

MYRNA: Yes, of course. But not so soon. Don't you know how to be nice to a woman?

STEVE: So you want to be nice, do you?

MYRNA: A woman wants to know a man; she wants to be friends and learn to love him.

STEVE: You're not gonna be angry with me for this?

MYRNA: What do you mean?

STEVE: For carryin' you off like this.

MYRNA: Not at all. It is the custom among the Vichadas.

STEVE: Who are the Vichadas?

MYRNA: They're the South American Indians that I lived among. They would raid the villages of the enemy tribes and carry off their women. They made very good wives, mostly. Now and then there was one who wouldn't be tamed, and they would have to kill her.

STEVE: The men had more than one wife?

MYRNA: Oh, yes; a good warrior might have three or four.

STEVE: And the women obeyed them?

MYRNA: Of course they did—they had to.

STEVE: Well, I'm a good warrior, and you obey me and we'll get along fine.

MYRNA: Just be kind to me, as the Indians were to their women, and I'll love you.

STEVE: Okay, I'll be a good Indian.

MYRNA: Tell me about this queer-looking place.

STEVE: You were never in a bank before?

MYRNA: I was never in a city before. I know nothing about it, except what my father has told me. What is a bank?

STEVE: A bank is a place where people keep money.

MYRNA: My father explained to me about money but I couldn't understand it very well.

STEVE: You didn't have no money where you come from?

MYRNA: The Vichadas exchanged egret feathers for salt, fishhooks, and things they needed; but money— all that I knew was that father had some little round pieces of metal that he showed me. I thought they must be magic.

STEVE, *grinning:* They were. They would get you anything you wanted. Below here under the ground are great vaults where they hid billions of dollars. I used to work here so I know about it.

MYRNA: Tell me how you worked. What did you do?

STEVE: First I was a messenger boy; I had to leave school because my father died. My mother had eight kids to take care of, so I went to work. The bank asked the priest, and he said I was a good boy who came to Sunday school, so they gave me a job as a messenger. I ran all over this financial district carrying a little bag with stocks and bonds in it.

MYRNA: What are stocks and bonds?

STEVE: They're pieces of paper that show that people own this and that—the industries of the country, the great factories, and so on. You had shares of stock, and that meant you got part of the profits earned by that concern. You get that, baby?

MYRNA: I suppose I get it.

STEVE: There was the Stock Exchange where the stocks and bonds were sold, and every now and then they had panics, and it was a great time for a kid to be alive and see the excitement. I didn't get much in the way of wages, but I saw all these rich people that had the money and had everything they wanted, and I made up my mind that someday I was going to get my share, and Mom and the kids was going to have what they wanted. Down here in these vaults they had watchmen, and I got to know one of those fellows, and he was old and had to quit, and I asked for his job. They looked me up some more and decided that I was pretty young for a watchman but they would train me. So I got the job, and this is the way it was; you go down in an elevator, several stories underground, and you go through a great steel door that looks like the wall of a house, and then maybe you think you're in the vault, but you're not. You're only at the beginning of the entrance. That vault has the billions of dollars in it, y'unnerstan', and all the way around is a narrow passage a man can walk in, and can walk all the way round, all four sides of it. On the outside of that wall is another chamber all the way around, and that's full of enough poison gas to kill anybody who tries to bore through; and beyond that are great walls of concrete that you couldn't bore through if you wanted to. So it goes—all the tricks they thought up to make sure that nobody ever got in to steal that gold and the stocks and bonds. In the passage that's open and that a man could walk around I used to sit as a watchman eight hours every night. I come on at ten o'clock in the evening and I sat till six o'clock next morning. There was three relays of men, y'unnerstan', so there was someone keepin' watch all twenty-four hours a day. From the chair where I sat there was mirrors in front of me, so I never had to turn or move an inch,

I just looked in them mirrors; they was fixed so that you could see all the way around all four of the passages goin' around the big vault, and every fifteen minutes I had to get up and walk about ten feet and press a button, and then come back and sit in my chair and keep watch again, and if I didn't press that button at the end of the fifteen minutes there would be a buzzer that would wake me up, and if I didn't press the button within a minute after that buzzer sounded, then an alarm bell would ring out where the night watchman was, and he would press a button to call the police. So every night, year in and year out, I come and sat in that chair. And then I would go out in the daytime and I would see all the wonderful things in the city that you could have if you had money—and you couldn't have if you didn't have money. All the time that I sat in that chair I was trying to figure out some way that I could get into that vault and get some of the money. I would get me a mob—

MYRNA: What is a mob?

STEVE: Some fellows—and we would work out a way to break through that chamber of poison gas without gettin' killed, and we would find some way to get into that vault.

MYRNA: Couldn't you have let them in?

STEVE: I was locked in myself. They locked me in every night and I had to stay there 'til they let me out in the morning. All I had to do was to sit there and look in the mirror that was reflected from all the other mirrors that would have showed me if anybody had been movin' anywheres in that passage that went all around the four walls of the vault. And there I sat and I figured, and I couldn't figure no way that I could get into that place or get out of that place, and there wasn't any way I could get that gold or them stocks and bonds that belonged to the rich people.

MYRNA: Then what did you do?

STEVE: Well, there come this plague, Bio they called it, and people begun to die all around me. I thought, I'll go out into the country like the others; but then I thought no, they'll all be going out into the country and gettin' killed out there because they'll take the Bio with them. What I'll do will be to go down into my vault where nobody can get at me. There wasn't anybody to stop me any more, y'unnerstan'; nobody had any use for stocks and bonds or for gold. You could have helped yourself, but what good would it do you? I had found a place where I could get some food. It was a wholesale grocery warehouse, and it had mineral water and all the things that I needed to keep alive. There was a guy who was livin' there, but I shot him and got what I wanted, and I went back to live in my vault where it was safe. You see, in this place I can lock myself in; I got the combination and nobody can get at me, and here I stay. I'm taking care of myself.

MYRNA: What for?

STEVE: I dunno what for; I'm just keeping alive. The worst thing is the loneliness, and I said to myself, if only I could get me a girl. So I went out looking for a girl—I have been looking ten years for a girl—and now I got one, and Jesus, am I glad!

MYRNA: You treat me right, and I will be a good girl. I'll cook your food, clean up your place, and take care of you.

STEVE: That'll be fine, but I'll make darn sure you don't run out on me.

MYRNA: I don't want to run out on you. I want to have a husband. I want to have a baby.

STEVE: You want a baby?

MYRNA: Surely I want a baby. Doesn't every woman want babies?

STEVE: I never met one before who wanted them—or anyhow, she wouldn't say it.

MYRNA: Among the Vichadas every girl wanted to have a baby just as soon as she could, and she didn't mind saying so. Life was pretty uncertain among those people and babies were important.

STEVE: Didn't you never have a baby? A big girl like you?

MYRNA: My father told me to wait because I might come back among the white people, and I did what my father told me. Among the Vichadas the woman always obeys the man; first her father and then her husband.

STEVE: That's the way it oughta be.

MYRNA: You treat me right, love me, and I'll stay here with you.

STEVE: I'm sorry I had to shoot your brother.

MYRNA: It was his own fault; he should have done what you said.

STEVE: That bullet went through his shoulder—it won't kill him. It will heal up quick.

MYRNA: We are used to wounds in the jungle. The men had to hunt, and it was hard getting a living.

STEVE: What did they hunt with?

MYRNA: Mostly bows and arrows.

STEVE: Must have been hard gettin' a living with them.

MYRNA: Oh, no. They could shoot well. We could kill even the tapirs, which were huge animals. Then we smoked and dried the meat.

STEVE: Funny kind of life for a white girl.

MYRNA: I lived among those people, did what they did, and believed what they believed. I guess I believe most of it still.

STEVE: You never wore any kind of clothes but them?

MYRNA: No one had any other kind, except that we

wove cloaks of long grasses. We needed them when the rains came. The rains poured down in torrents, and at night everything was wet and chilly.

STEVE: Say, but you look pretty to a guy who hasn't seen a girl in ten years! What's that red feather you got in your hair?

MYRNA: That's a macaw feather. That's to keep the evil spirits away.

STEVE: That what it does?

MYRNA: That's what the Vichadas say it does. My Daddy says there are no evil spirits, but I thought it couldn't do any harm to be on the safe side.

STEVE: And what's that little box you've got danglin'?

MYRNA: That's where I keep my paint.

STEVE: Paint? What do you do with paint?

MYRNA: I paint my face and my body. That's for great occasions.

STEVE: What kind of occasions?

MYRNA: Well, for example, love.

STEVE: You paint yourself for love? That's called lipstick here.

MYRNA: Women are alike, I guess.

STEVE: Where do you paint yourself?

MYRNA: Many places.

STEVE: How about painting yourself now?

MYRNA: It takes time. I must paint all the symbols of love. I paint a picture of the baby I expect to have. All that makes it come out right. My father calls it black magic.

STEVE: What color's the paint?

MYRNA: It's black, of course.

STEVE: Couldn't you get any prettier color than that?

MYRNA: It isn't a question of color, it's a question of magic. The witch doctor dances and treats the stuff and makes it powerful. We had a wonderful witch doctor named Golubu, and everything he did was right. He protected the tribe from the demons of the river, and the demons of the jungle, and all the other demons; he gave the tribe victory whenever the head-hunters from the other enemy tribes came and tried to kill our warriors.

STEVE: Jesus, what a crazy lot of stuff! Let me see the paint.

MYRNA, *unfastening the box and opening it:* We take some of the paint on your finger, like this—*she suits the action to the words*—and then we use it to paint ourselves and our husbands

STEVE, *lifting the box and smelling it:* Ugh, kind of rancid stuff!

MYRNA: We don't mind the smell, we think about the magic.

STEVE: Well, it's all right with me. You can paint symbols all over yourself if that'll make you happy. Would it be right for you to give me a kiss, maybe?

MYRNA: That would be all right, I guess, but you must be gentle and polite.

*Steve moves over on the bench, puts his arms around her, kisses her on the lips. She puts her arms around him, and with the finger on which she has put the curare she scratches him with a fingernail.*

STEVE, *starting back angrily:* Ouch! What the hell? You scratched me.

MYRNA: But of course.

STEVE, *in fury, starting to draw his gun:* You little bitch!

MYRNA: But I had to scratch you.

STEVE: Had to! What do you mean?

MYRNA: That's part of the love ritual.

STEVE: The hell you say!

MYRNA: For me to be your wife we have to have the blood ceremony.

STEVE: What's that?

MYRNA: I scratch you in the back of the neck and I

draw a little blood. I thought you would scratch me and do the same.

STEVE: I never heard of such a crazy thing.

MYRNA: Well, how could I know? I thought everybody knew about the marriage ceremony of the mixing of the blood.

STEVE: Like hell! That's all nonsense!

MYRNA: You must understand that I have lived all my life among the Indians, and I only know what they know. I thought you would know of the mixing of the blood.

STEVE: Oh! So I have to scratch you till *you* bleed?

MYRNA: I have a drop of your blood on my hand, and you have a drop of my blood on your hand, and we rub them together, and so we become one, and I belong to you for life.

STEVE: Christ, what an idea! It sounds loony to me. In this country when you get married you go to a priest and he marries you. But there ain't any more priests, at least not that I know of.

MYRNA: Well, then we had better get married by the Vichada ceremony.

STEVE: It's okay by me if it makes you happy. I'll scratch your neck. *He starts to lean toward her but stops before he has touched her. A long pause while he manifests confusion of mind.* I feel queer!

MYRNA: Queer? What do you mean?

STEVE: Sort of dizzy.

MYRNA: You're excited. It's because you're in love.

STEVE: Maybe so, but I—

MYRNA: Try to calm yourself.

STEVE: Jesus! I can't. I'm—what have you done to me?

MYRNA: Done to you? What could I do to you?

STEVE: You scratched me.

MYRNA: A tiny scratch. What could a tiny scratch do to a strong man like you?

STEVE, *excitedly:* What's that stuff? You had it on your fingernail.

MYRNA: It's perfectly harmless. It's nothing but the juice of a plant that the natives squeeze out and boil until it becomes a paste. It wouldn't hurt a baby; it wouldn't hurt a fly.

STEVE: I tell you I'm dizzy. I'm going—you've done something to me!

MYRNA: What would I do? I wouldn't do anything to the man I mean to love and marry. You're imagining things.

STEVE: No, I'm not. I'm growing dizzy. I'm going— *He stammers vague phrases.* I . . . I want . . . I can't . . .

*He starts moving his hand as if with a desperate effort toward the pocket where he has the gun. The effect of curare is upon the nerves; it prevents the coordination between the brain and the muscles. Steve knows that he wants to do something, but he can't bring himself to do it. His hand will not respond. He succeeds in getting the gun out of his pocket, with great distress of both mind and body. He starts to raise the gun. At that moment Myrna leaps and grasps his wrist, turns it around, and tears the gun from his hand; then she steps back with the gun. She doesn't know how to move the safety catch, but looks at it.*

STEVE, *staggering toward her:* You bitch! You, you—
*He rises to come toward her but reels, staggers, and suddenly collapses into a heap on the ground. The curare acts slowly at first, takes a few seconds to manifest itself, but its final effect is sudden, like a stroke of lightning. The man is dead. Myrna knows all about the effects of curare; she has killed thousands of animals with it, and now, with an expression of rage, she goes over to the man and kicks him two or three times.*

MYRNA: Beast!

*In a matter-of-fact fashion she proceeds to ransack the premises. She takes one of the sleeping blankets and spreads it on the floor. She lays the pistol on it, and then gathers up the cans of food and the clothing. She discovers a small hand mirror, gazes into it with delight, making plain that she has never seen one before. She studies herself from all possible angles, smiles into it, tries to see the back of her head, the side of her head, etc. Then she discovers a comb; this, too, she has never seen before, and she amuses herself by combing her hair and studying the effects of the procedure. She tries the effect of different hair-dos. At intervals she sits gazing at the body, gloating and occasionally breaking into a chuckle. She puts the comb and mirror among the treasures on the blanket. She gets a siphon of vichy water, sees that it is water and wants a drink. She tips the spout up to her mouth but no water comes. She shakes it but doesn't know how to make it come; finally she puts the siphon in with the other treasures. When she has collected all the objects that interest her she ties up the four corners of the blanket, picks it up, puts it carefully over her shoulder, and goes out by the door at right.*

CURTAIN

SCENE III: *The corner of Broad and Wall Streets as in Scene I.*

*As the curtain rises Angell and Bob are seen seated on the pavement. Bob has not put any dressing on his wound for they have nothing to dress it with. Blood has run down but has dried, and the bleeding has stopped. He is gazing up and down the street. Angell has his head in his hands.*

BOB: The time is passing and she does not come.

ANGELL: God help her!

BOB. We *must* hunt for her!

ANGELL: I hope she will not make him kill her.

BOB: I can't forgive myself!

ANGELL: He will probably lock her up and do his best to keep her from escaping. He may even put handcuffs on her.

BOB: What are handcuffs?

ANGELL: They are a device made of steel used by the police. They are like two bracelets and are put over the wrists to hold the two hands together. He may even put leg irons on her to keep her from moving.

BOB: If only I had had any idea that such men existed in your civilized world!

ANGELL: I should have known that a girl would be a desired object. One of us should have hidden and used the blowgun on him. But it's too late now.

BOB: We *must* hunt for her!

ANGELL: It's impossible to hunt in this jungle of buildings. Look at them! In any one building there may be a thousand rooms. There are even places underground; huge caverns, divided into many compartments, and she might be in any one of them.

BOB: What a hell of a place!

ANGELL: The people here had got used to it and would have thought the jungles were a hell of a place. In fact they did.

BOB: We can go crazy thinking about what may be happening to her.

ANGELL: We must not let ourselves go crazy. Myrna is strong and clever, and she may find a way to outwit that fellow. He may lock her up, but he must open the door sometime. He may chain her, but if he sleeps with her he cannot keep her chained always; sooner or later she will find a way to get hold of the gun or a knife. It may well be that she is stronger than he.

BOB: She said she would use curare on him, but how can she do it?

ANGELL: There is a story she has heard—of the Mangaruna woman who was captured in battle, brought in, and made the wife of one of the sub-chiefs of the Vichadas. The woman put curare under her fingernail, scratched him, and he died. Before he died he was able to stab her to death; but he was dead. Myrna knows that story, and she knows how long it takes for the poison to take effect; she will manage to keep out of his way that long. I would pray if I knew how to. What you must do is to keep yourself calm and not give yourself a fever with that wound.

BOB: Tell me, what sort of man could this be?

ANGELL: He must have been a gangster. We had bred

that type in every city of America before I came away.

BOB: What is a gangster?

ANGELL: He's a man who lives by preying upon the weakness of other men. Laws were passed forbidding gambling, the selling of dope, and other offenses, but men wanted to gamble, they wanted to have prostitutes, they wanted to indulge their vices, and the catering to these vices became a trade, one of the most profitable businesses in the community. The gangsters throve, multiplied, and grew rich.

BOB: You were supposed to have laws; couldn't they be enforced?

ANGELL: It was impossible to enforce the laws because the gangsters had the money and they would pay the local police and the public authorities not to interfere. It was a condition with which everybody was familiar, but no one knew what to do about it.

BOB: There was something wrong with a civilization that permitted such things.

ANGELL: There was something wrong with every civilization that has ever existed upon this earth, and they all destroyed themselves sooner or later.

BOB: Then civilization is really a disease.

ANGELL: The philosophers and sociologists and the learned gentlemen argued about it. Some said it was because our material progress had exceeded our moral progress. We invented huge machines for producing wealth, but we did not find a just way to distribute the wealth. We created terrible means of destruction, but we did not have the moral force to control ourselves, and we were not fit to be trusted with such weapons. There were other learned persons who said that the trouble lay in the economic basis upon which civilizations were built. In the jungles, as you know, nobody owns the land; any one of the Vichadas could go out and hunt game. If he shot a tapir, there was no private ownership of that tapir. The whole tribe came running out to carve it up and save the meat, to bring firewood and build the fires and tend them, and smoke and dry the meat and put it away in safe places, and the meat was divided up and everybody had what he wanted. That is the basis upon which the jungle people live. No member of the tribe preyed upon any other, no one killed another. When they wanted to do any killing they went out and killed the members of some other tribe. That may not be an ideal form of human existence, but at least it is one that can go on forever. But when you build a great city like this and allow some few of the men to grow rich, and to hold economic power over the mass of the people, you have a form of society that is always in convulsions, and will always be destroying itself.

Bob: You should have told me about all this. I would not have brought my sister to such a place if I had known it.

ANGELL: I did not realize what it would mean for a modern society to disintegrate and for its weapons of destruction to be left in the hands of anyone who chose to use them. Apparently there is no longer any law in New York City, and it may well be that there is no law anywhere in the United States, or perhaps even in the civilized world.

BOB: You think the enemy may have been destroyed also?

ANGELL: It seems pretty certain that if he had not been destroyed he would have come here by now. It is possible to live in the streets apparently—for we are still alive. Since the enemy has not come, we have to suppose that we used on him the same weapons that he used on us. We all had them, of course; there was no way to keep scientific knowledge from being spread, and there was no way to keep each separate nation from creating new means of destruction.

BOB: The more I hear about it, the more I think that I prefer the head-hunters. They only kill one man at a time, and they save the women and children. *Wildly.* And we just sit here!

ANGELL: We have to be here if Myrna comes to look for us. If she doesn't find us she will think we have wandered off or been killed, and we may never get together again.

BOB: We shall have to have some food and water.

ANGELL: I'll go look for them. You must let your shoulder rest. I have no dressing to put on it, and we shall just have to put our hopes in Mother Nature.

BOB: I feel all right now, Father.

ANGELL: After you get a wound the pain diminishes, but fever may begin. You must positively rest.

BOB: I'll sit here and hold my blowgun ready for the next gangster.

ANGELL, *rising:* I will go have a look on the other side of Broadway.

BOB: You're taking your life in your hands.

ANGELL: I'll be careful. *He looks, first right and then left, and suddenly exclaims in excitement:* Here she comes! Here she comes! *As Bob starts to rise:* Sit down! You must not exert yourself.

MYRNA, *calling offstage:* Yoo hoo!

ANGELL: I will go and meet her. *He calls:* Yoo hoo!

*He exits; after a sufficient time they re-enter, she in front and he carrying the bundle in the blanket.*

BOB, *in excitement:* You got away!

MYRNA: I killed him.

BOB: How?

MYRNA: Didn't I tell you I'd get him with curare?

BOB: How did you do it?

MYRNA: I managed to get some under my fingernail and I gave him a good deep scratch in the neck.

ANGELL: Why didn't he kill you?

MYRNA: I had made up a fancy story. I told him that the curare was what we painted our faces with on our wedding night, and he believed me.

ANGELL: Did he do you any harm?

MYRNA: No, he was quite polite.

ANGELL: Thank God!

MYRNA: I told him I would love him. I told him I would make him a good wife.

ANGELL: I figured out that you would scratch him with the curare, but I couldn't figure out how you would keep him from shooting you before the stuff took effect.

MYRNA: I had time to think about it while he was walking me to the place; me in front and him behind with the gun, telling me to turn right or left. I decided to tell him that the scratching was a blood ceremony; he was to scratch me and we were to mingle our blood, and that would be our marriage.

ANGELL: And you got him to believe that?

MYRNA: Why shouldn't he believe it? He doesn't know anything about the Vichadas, and everything I told him was strange.

ANGELL: Tearing his skin with your fingernails was dangerous. You might have pulled your own skin away from your fingernail and got the poison into your own blood.

MYRNA: I had to take the chance. I surely wasn't going to be his woman if I could help it. He's a beast, and he shot my brother! How are you, Bob?

BOB: I'm going to be all right. The bullet came through.

ANGELL: We must go down to the river right away and wash that curare from under your fingernail.

MYRNA: I brought some water with me; at least it looks like water, but I can't get it to come out. *She stoops to the bundle, opens it, and takes out the siphon of vichy water.* I tilted it every which way but I can't get it out.

ANGELL, *smiling:* It's a little trick. You have to press this lever down, and you mustn't press it too hard or it shoots.

MYRNA: Shoots? Does it hurt?

ANGELL: No, not hurts but squirts. *He takes the siphon, holds the nozzle over her fingers, and lets a little water out, a few drops at a time, while she rubs the curare away.* Now we can have a drink. *He gives each one of them a drink by holding the nozzle over their mouths and squirting the water carefully. He gives Myrna a quick dousing, and they all laugh. He takes a drink himself.*

BOB: What strange water! It bites.

ANGELL: It's charged water; it has a gas in it.

BOB: What was it used for?

ANGELL: It gave a pleasant tang to other drinks.

MYRNA, *sorting out her treasures and holding them up:*
Here's the gun. When I got it away from him, I tried to
shoot him, but it wouldn't work.

ANGELL: There's a little safety catch here. You had better let me carry it. We'll not be so helpless next time.

MYRNA: Here are cartridges, loads of them, and here
is a comb. I have combed my hair, and you can see how
pretty it is. Daddy, do you think I look pretty to the
white men?

ANGELL: You seem to have pleased them so far.

BOB: Don't forget you had a proposal of marriage from
the guy from Brooklyn.

MYRNA: I don't want him because he ran away. I want
a man who will stand and defend me. I want to find one
so that I can have a baby. When we get settled I want
to have lots of babies.

ANGELL: Let us hope so. The world will need them.

MYRNA: If I have babies, they will be brothers and
sisters. Bob will have to find a girl, and then his children
and mine will be cousins. Can cousins marry?

ANGELL: Yes, and that will be all right.

MYRNA: Here's a good knife. I was thinking that perhaps I should cut off that gangster's head and smoke it over a fire and shrink it. I really have earned it.

ANGELL: Yes, but that wouldn't help you with a man in the white country. It would frighten all of them.

MYRNA: Well, I may have to frighten them a little bit too. *She lifts up the well-worn coat.* And here is a coat; look how wonderful! It has sleeves, and how beautifully it is sewed! I never saw anything like it.

BOB: You took a chance bringing it.

MYRNA: I figured the man had been wearing it, and he wasn't dead; so it can't have the Bio in it. Daddy, look at this. *She puts the coat on.* That old black woman was shocked because I haven't enough clothes on. Do you think I should wear this?

ANGELL: Forget the black woman. When I left America, women at the beaches were wearing bathing suits not much bigger than what you have. We'll call you a bathing beauty; you can be Miss America of this year.

MYRNA: Look, Daddy, all these things! I suppose this is what you call canned food.

ANGELL: Yes.

MYRNA, *reading:* Peaches. What are they?

ANGELL: It's a kind of fruit; you'll find it very pleasant.

MYRNA: And soup. What is mock turtle soup?

ANGELL: It's supposed to taste like turtle, but it isn't.

MYRNA: I would like to find some made of anaconda meat.

ANGELL: This meat will be from a cow, a creature of which I drew you pictures. There is some canned milk, and that also will be from a cow.

MYRNA: Oh, how good! Let us have some. I have never been so hungry that I can remember. And poor Bob will need nourishment. How are you feeling, Bob?

BOB: I feel hollow inside, and some cow milk and cow soup would suit me fine.

*They squat comfortably on the pavement.*

MYRNA: How do you get things out of these cans, Daddy?

ANGELL: It needs what is called a can opener. *He looks in the pile of stuff in the blanket.* Here is one. *He shows them how to open the cans, and they watch with delight.*

MYRNA: How clever! And these lovely little pans, Daddy, what are they?

ANGELL: They are made of aluminum and are light and easy to clean.

MYRNA: And these little shiny cups? I never saw anything so pretty.

ANGELL: Well, the people up here would think that our calabashes and gourds were pretty.

*He apportions the food, and they proceed to eat.*

MYRNA: How wonderful, Daddy! I never ate anything that tasted so good. Are you sure it won't have the Bio?

ANGELL: This canning must have been done before the virus struck. Your gangster was eating it and he was alive.

MYRNA: He shot another man and took the food away from him; now it's our turn. You don't believe in my red feather, Daddy, but you surely ought to after today.

ANGELL: At least I believe that your red feather doesn't do any harm; and it may please the men.

MYRNA: Oh, I've surely got to find a husband, Daddy. Where shall we go?

ANGELL: What I want to do first is to get Bob and all these things into the boat. He can lie there and rest. He ought to sleep as much as possible. You and I can take the boat out to the middle of the river and let the tide carry it up and down, wherever it wants to, and we can watch and see how things look. It will be safer out there, and we will have time to figure out how to find you a husband.

MYRNA: Oh, Daddy, I am so excited! I must find a man, and a nice one—one that I won't have to kill so soon!

CURTAIN

# Act Three

SCENE I: *In front of Grant's Tomb on Riverside Drive. The stage represents a paved walk in front of the Drive, and the backdrop shows the Tomb and the steps leading up to it. The grass at the sides has grown up with tall weeds. Upstage near center are two patches of loose earth set in frames about sixteen inches square and a couple of inches high; under each is concealed a trapdoor.*

*There are entrances to the stage at right and left. The entrance at right leads to the steep embankment going down to the Hudson River. The entrance at left leads to the main drive. These features are not visible but are referred to in the course of the act.*

*As the curtain rises the stage is vacant. Angell, Bob, and Myrna come on, all three carrying their blowguns. Angell has the automatic stuck in his loincloth. Bob's wound is obviously healing. Myrna still wears her red feather. Angell is carrying a small bundle. They gaze around them with curiosity.*

ANGELL: That was a hard climb for a wounded man. Sit down, Bob, and rest.

BOB: Really, Father, I'm quite all right now.

ANGELL: I'm the doctor, and I tell you to rest.

BOB: All right.

*He sits on the pavement. Angell puts his bundle down.*

MYRNA: Oh, what a lovely spot, Daddy! *She gazes off right.* That great still river, and those beautiful cliffs!

ANGELL: Those are the Palisades. They were quite famous. In the old days there was an amusement park over there which would have delighted you still more.

MYRNA: I wouldn't have needed any amusement, I would have just wanted to see the people, and how they were dressed and how they behaved.

BOB: This is a place for a meal.

ANGELL: Only one thing worries me—that other boat we saw down there.

MYRNA: But there was nobody in it.

ANGELL: They may have been hiding to see who we were, and where we would go. They might carry off our things; they might even take the boat.

MYRNA: I'll sit where I can look down and keep watch. *She goes off right.*

BOB: Well, what do you think we should do now?

ANGELL: It seems to me that we are about through with New York. The Rockefeller Institute is deserted. My bank is closed and I can't get any money, and I wouldn't have any use for it if I could. Columbia University has a magnificent library, but we dare not go inside or touch any of the books.

BOB: And so what?

ANGELL: I suggest that we follow the example of Henry Hudson, the old-time explorer, and sail up the river. We won't get to the Indies, as he expected, and we don't want to, anyhow. We might find some good farm land where we could plant early vegetables, and get radishes, lettuce, and young onions before cold weather comes.

BOB: If we could get the seeds.

ANGELL: There might be some plants with seeds still left in them. There is pretty sure to be game. It's interesting to see how the fish have come back to the river, now that industry is no longer discharging chemicals into it.

BOB: We must stop somewhere and get ready for cold weather.

ANGELL: We have to build a hut and chink the crevices with mud or clay.

MYRNA, *calling off right:* There are people starting to climb the hill. I think they are from the other boat.

ANGELL, *calling:* What sort of people?

MYRNA: There are three of them; one is a big tall man with a beard. I can't make out whether the others are men or women. Yes, one of them has a light beard. They all wear some sort of coats that are hairy.

ANGELL: Are they armed?

MYRNA: I can't be sure; they are carrying what look like poles.

ANGELL: I will come. *To Bob:* You wait here. Be ready with your blowgun.

*He hurries off right, and almost immediately Myrna comes on.*

MYRNA: He says I'm to hide in the bushes; they must not see me.

BOB: All right, hide. I'll not let them near you.

MYRNA: Watch out for yourself too. *She exits left.*

ANGELL, *offstage:* Hello! Who are you?

LEIF, *calling from distance, right:* We are good people. We mean harm to no man.

ANGELL: Where do you come from?

LEIF: A long distance—from Iceland by way of Greenland and Labrador.

ANGELL: What are those things you carry?

LEIF: They are harpoons. They are for walruses, not for humans.

ANGELL: You will not find walruses up here.

LEIF: We could not tell what we might find, but we will be friends with friendly men.

*As this dialogue goes on, the voice of Leif comes nearer and nearer.*

ANGELL: Have you got the Bio?

LEIF: We do not know what that is.

ANGELL: I mean the plague that killed people.

LEIF: We are not dead; that is all we can say.

ANGELL: That's true for us also; but let us not come close together.

LEIF: That suits us very well. We have had a hard journey, and we should be glad to have friends.

ANGELL: We too have had a hard journey. We are Americans, but we have been living in the jungles of South America.

LEIF: Ho! Ho! The North Pole meets the Equator! We shall have tales to tell one another.

*Angell comes on slowly, backward, and the other three follow him; they keep about fifteen feet apart. Leif is an old giant, lean and battered by hardship. His gray hair and beard are long and wild. He is clad in a garment made of skins with long hair. His two grandchildren wear the same kind of garments. The grandson is twenty or so and has a light brown beard. The girl is younger, and her hair is golden and long. The younger man carries a bundle slung over one shoulder.*

ANGELL: Let us stand this far apart for the safety of all of us. This is my son, who has been wounded by a gangster; but his wound is healing.

LEIF: A gangster, you say? Then we are indeed in America! From your costume it is evident that you have come from the south.

ANGELL: From far, far in the south. From the jungles near the head waters of the Orinoco River. We paddled in a dugout down those waters, infested with crocodiles and deadly fish and serpents. We reached the sea and found only emptiness and loneliness. We fitted ourselves a small sailboat and sailed through the chain of islands of the Caribbean, and through the Bahamas to Florida; then we came up the inland channel through the Carolinas, and from there bit by bit, when weather on the open sea permitted, to New York which was my former home.

LEIF: You are a man of education, I take it.

ANGELL: I was a botanist employed by the Rockefeller Institute. And you too, I take it, are a scholar.

LEIF: I was a government official in Iceland, and the virus reached there. It has reached everywhere, apparently. Word came from Europe that people were dying wholesale.

ANGELL: Ah! Then we must have given it to the enemy, even as he gave it to us.

LEIF: Even so. An eye for an eye and a tooth for a tooth.

Only it was the eyes of millions of innocent people, and their teeth as well.

ANGELL: You speak excellent English, I note.

LEIF: I was known as a translator of our ancient Eddas. You know our Eddas, perhaps?

ANGELL: I have heard of them, but my time for reading poetry has been limited.

LEIF: I saw people dying all around me, and I said to my family, we will go back to the ways of our fore-fathers. We will take to the sea. We got a boat and put our belongings into it and set out. These two young people, my grandchildren, are all that survived. We sailed as far as Labrador and lived there for many years, hunting the sea creatures with our harpoons and the caribou with what ammunition we had left. When we sailed again, all but we three were lost in raging storms. My friends, it was a journey of hardships, like those in our Eddic lay, "The Lamentation of Gudrun."

> Father and mother,
> and four brothers
> on the wide sea
> the winds and death played with;
> the billows beat
> on the bulwark boards.
>
> Alone must I array them,
> alone must my hands deal

with their departing;
and all this was
in one season's wearing,
and none was left
for love or solace.

ANGELL: We were born to hard times, my friend. We have witnessed calamities without parallel in history, I believe.

LEIF: In the poem entitled "Völuspá," meaning "The Prophecy of the Sybil," it is written:

The sun knew not
where she had a dwelling;
the moon knew not
what power he possessed;
the stars knew not
where they had a station.

ANGELL: I too have had sorrow. I saw my wife dying, and she begged me with tears in her eyes to take the children and save them. People were falling in the streets of our wretched little town on the Orinoco River.

LEIF: In the "Hávamál," "The Speech of the High One," the oldest of all our Eddic lays, it tells:

Cattle die,
kindred die,
we ourselves also die;

but the fair fame
never dies
of him that has earned it.

ANGELL: I perceive that you are good people and honest; a man who has been interested in translating such verses is worthy of friendship.

LEIF: It is true of us; but, alas, it is not always true. The Germans had a song which said that evil men have no songs. Singing that song, they invaded our Scandinavian lands and enslaved the people.

ANGELL: Absit omen, as the ancient Romans used to say. Let us make a pact together and keep the peace.

LEIF: It is done, but let us not shake hands on it, because we might be bringing the infection to you.

ANGELL: Or we to you. I introduce my son, whose name is Bob.

BOB: I am pleased to meet you, sir.

LEIF: This is my granddaughter Elfrida, and this is my grandson Eric. Eric, heilsaðu manninum.

ERIC: Segðu honum ég voni að við verðum vinir.

LEIF: He says he hopes you will be friends.

BOB: Surely.

LEIF: This is my granddaughter Elfrida. Nú færðu loksins ástæðu til að læra ensku, Elfrida. *To the others:*

I am telling her that at last she has a reason for studying English.

ELFRIDA: Segðu honum ég geri það með ánægju og hann megi vera kennari minn.

LEIF: She says she will be glad to do so, and you will be her teacher.

BOB: To be sure I will.

LEIF: I have had great trouble in getting these young people to study.

ANGELL: In the jungles of eastern Colombia my children had no books to study. They know only what I have been able to teach them by voice. I wrote words for them and taught them their letters; so now they are very proud that they are able to read the names on buildings and the labels on a can of beans or beef soup.

MYRNA, *calling off left:* There's an automobile coming. *Sound of an automobile is heard in the distance, off left.*

ANGELL: Stay hidden, Myrna.

*The sound has grown rapidly louder. Angell turns so that his automatic is hidden from the approaching car; he quickly shifts it, sticking it into the loincloth at his back. The five persons, standing in two groups, watch the car, which stops with a screeching of brakes immediately off left.*

BUGSIE, *calling off left:* Stick 'em up! This is a holdup! Put up your hands, or I'll drill you through!

*He comes onstage quickly, holding a tommygun in instant readiness; he is a thin-faced, nervous young fellow, looks as menacing as he can, and speaks in a voice meant to terrify. He is followed by Red, another tough-looking youth, who carries an automatic. The two stop some distance from the company.*

BUGSIE: Stick 'em up! Can't you hear me?

LEIF, *mildly:* My friend, you need not be so violent; we are peaceable people and mean no harm to anyone.

BUGSIE: What's them things you got in your hand?

LEIF: These are harpoons; they are meant for walruses, not for humans.

BUGSIE: Put 'em down, I say.

LEIF: These young people do not understand English. Hann segir okkur að leggja þau niður. Við verðum að hlýða.

*The three of them carefully lay the harpoons on the ground.*

BUGSIE: Put your hands up!

LEIF: Upp með hendurnar! *The three obey.*

BUGSIE, *addressing Angell:* What's them pipes you fellows got?

ANGELL: These are electro-magnetic resonators.

BUGSIE: What the hell!

ANGELL: They are meant to help and not to harm. They are instruments by which we test the existence of those alpha and gamma rays which have been bringing wholesale death to people all over the world.

BUGSIE: What you givin' us?

ANGELL: The resonators are my own invention and represent one of the most important discoveries of our time.

BUGSIE: Well, drop 'em!

ANGELL: If you don't mind, we will lay them down gently, for they are easily ruined. *He and Bob lay the blowguns carefully on the ground.*

BUGSIE: Now put up your hands, and do it quick, or this gun will cut you in half! *Angell and Bob raise their hands.*

ANGELL: You are making a mistake, my friend. My son and I are travelers who have come a long way in a small boat, and we have nothing of any value to you. As for these other people, let the old gentleman tell you about them.

LEIF: We have come all the way from Iceland, through some of the coldest seas of the world. We have escaped after great hardship and are glad to have saved our lives. We have nothing of any use to you.

BUGSIE: That's a girl, ain't it?

LEIF: Yes, that's a girl.

BUGSIE: That's what we want. Tell her to come with us.

LEIF: Oh, surely you cannot mean that! She is my granddaughter.

BUGSIE: Granddaughter or grandmother, I don't care. Tell her to come.

LEIF: I will tell her what you say. Hann segir þú eigir að koma með honum.

ELFRIDA: Ég vil það ekki.

LEIF: She says she will not.

BUGSIE: Tell her she will come and no nonsense. If she doesn't, I will shoot her granddaddy full of holes.

LEIF: I will not tell her that. You may go ahead and shoot.

BUGSIE: As you please, old man. *He levels the gun.*

ANGELL: One moment, please, my friend. You must understand this situation. If you take this girl you will be bringing your own life to an end.

BUGSIE: How do you get that?

ANGELL: We have just been testing these people with our electro-magnetic resonators. All three of them are so infected with alpha and gamma rays that it is sure death to touch them. Have you not noticed that we have been standing apart? I would not lay a hand upon one of those three people for all the treasures in the city of New York.

BUGSIE: There was a sucker born every minute, mister; but I ain't one of them.

ANGELL: It's too bad you're not familiar with scientific terms, so that I could make you understand the operation of this apparatus.

BUGSIE: It looks like nothing but a little wooden pipe.

ANGELL: Quite so; but inside are fluorescent particles that concentrate and intensify the electronic emanations. I have been working for more than twenty years to perfect this process.

BUGSIE: How do you tell about it?—the danger, I mean.

ANGELL: There are various ways in which you can detect the sensitivity. For one, with your tongue. If you touch it to the end of this pipe, you will almost certainly feel the vibrations which this girl has imparted.

BUGSIE: Yah! A likely trick. Ketch me stickin' my tongue on your monkey business.

ANGELL: It is every man's privilege to reject the benefits of science.

BUGSIE: Benefits? Ha, ha, ha! You guys that have destroyed most of the world!

ANGELL: It happens that I am not one of those guys. I am one who was trying to build up and not to destroy. Let me tell you, you may feel the effects from this powerful instrument even from being close to it.

BUGSIE: Where will I feel it?

ANGELL: In various places. Generally the vibrations first affect the back of the neck. You may feel a sharp stinging sensation.

BUGSIE: Christ, what you guys think up! Let me tell you, buddy, you can't gyp me with your smooth talk. I want that girl. I've been without a girl for so many years I forgot what one looks like, and I'd just as soon be dead as go any longer. *To Leif:* Grandpa, I want that girl! Tell her to come. If she don't come, first there will be one shot for you, then there will be one for your boy, and then there will be one for this scientific guy, then there will be one for his boy. One, two, three, four shots. It's up to her to say how many. Tell her to come! *He lifts the tommygun and aims it; then with a wild cry he clasps one hand to the back of his neck.* I'm shot! What the hell is that?

ANGELL: That's the electro-magnetic resonation I've been telling you about.

RED, *looking off left and pointing in excitement:* There's somebody hidin' in them bushes!

*Bugsie whirls and starts to aim the gun off left. Angell whips his automatic from behind his back and fires three times at Bugsie, who collapses. At the same moment Bob stoops and picks up the blowgun and blows a dart into the back of Red's neck. Red screams and runs off left. Offstage he is heard to scream again.*

LEIF: Very clever indeed! Why didn't you shoot the second one?

ANGELL: There is no need. Bob gave him a dart from the blowgun, and my daughter has given him another. He will not run more than a hundred yards.

LEIF: What is this strange weapon?

ANGELL: It is a blowgun used by the Indians of the South American jungle. The thin darts are tipped with curare, a quick-acting poison.

LEIF: I have heard of it.

ANGELL, *as Myrna comes on left:* This is my daughter Myrna.

LEIF: Oh, a lovely girl! And a remarkably accurate markswoman.

ANGELL: She learned to shoot birds out of the treetops when she was a little child. She has shot and killed deer with her blowgun at fifty yards. Myrna, this is a learned gentleman from Iceland.

MYRNA: I am honored to meet you, sir.

LEIF: I congratulate you upon your skill. You have saved all our lives. This is my grandson Eric.

Myrna: How do you do?

Leif: And this is my granddaughter Elfrida.

Myrna: I'm pleased to meet you.

Leif: Hér færðu ástæðu til að læra að tala ensku, Eric! *To Myrna:* I'm telling him that now he has a reason for learning to speak English.

Eric: Spurðu hana hvort hún vilji vera kennari minn.

Leif: He asks if you will be his teacher.

Myrna: Indeed I will. Tell him I may also be willing to become his wife.

Leif: Ho! ho! How delightful! I had the thought the moment I saw you! And so did he, I've no doubt.

Angell, *interposing:* Among the Vichada Indians, where this child was brought up, it is the custom of the girls to speak frankly of their desires. I neglected to caution her as to the difference of custom in the white world.

Leif: It would have been a shame to destroy such spontaneity. *To Eric:* Hún segir það gæti verið að hún vildi verða konan þín.

Eric: Segðu henni mér dytti ekki í hug að neita.

Leif: He says he could not imagine refusing.

Bob: Speak for me also. Tell Elfrida that I very much want to have a wife. And I am no gangster.

LEIF: I will tell her. Hann segir sig langi mikið til að eignast konu og hann sé enginn stigamaður.

ELFRIDA: Segðu honum að útlitið sé gott; og segðu honum að nú sé ég viss um að við séum í Ameríku. Þetta er alveg eins og í kvikmyndunum.

LEIF, *laughing heartily:* She says that your chances are good; and that she is sure now that we are in America, because it is exactly like the movies.

ANGELL: First a brush with the gangsters and then a love scene; but it will be different in one respect: there must be no embraces. We should wait a day or two to see if we are still alive.

LEIF, *addressing his grandchildren:* Hann segir að faðmlög komi ekki til mála, við verðum að bíða einn til tvo daga og sjá til hvort við verðum öll á lífi.

ELFRIDA: Segðu honum mér leiðist að vera ekki betur klædd.

LEIF: She says she regrets that she is not more properly dressed.

BOB: Tell her that I will take her on faith.

LEIF: Hann segist trúa þér.

ELFRIDA: Ég þakka honum fyrir það.

LEIF: She says she appreciates your trustfulness. Now let us put our minds upon more immediate matters. What is this place?

ANGELL: This is the tomb of General Grant, who commanded the victorious armies in America's great Civil War.

LEIF: I have read about him; and I see upon his monument the inscription "Let Us Have Peace."

ANGELL: He spoke those words immediately after the signing of the surrender. He was a fighting man who hated war.

LEIF: Alas, he would not be very happy in our time!

ANGELL: His words were engraved upon marble but not in the hearts of men; at least not in the hearts of our enemies, who believed in force.

LEIF: Both sides always say that they want peace, but they also want things which cannot be got without war. It appears that we are going to set about the founding of a new society. Let us see that the children are taught to practice cooperation and kindness. Tell me, my friends, have you any plans for the future?

ANGELL: We had talked it over and decided that we would follow in the wake of Henry Hudson, sailing up this broad and peaceful river. We can surely find some farm land which can be made to produce enough to eat. I think it likely that the game has multiplied and has lost its fear of men. Perhaps we shall find people, but our recent experiences suggest that the less we have to do with them the better.

LEIF: The survival of the fittest seems to have meant the gangsters in this unfortunate period.

ANGELL: Just so. By the coming of cold weather we must have some sort of shelter constructed—since it would be folly for us to enter any of the existing houses.

LEIF: With our forces doubled we can surely be equal to the task. This program suits us perfectly. We will sail our boats separately.

ANGELL: As it happens, we have had nothing to eat this morning, and perhaps you too might be interested in food. We have brought several cans along with us.

LEIF: We have had an adventure, more pleasant than the recent one. Down in the harbor we passed a small wrecked boat, its masts sticking up above the water. My capable grandson dived down and was able to get the hatch off the little craft, and what do you think came up?—sent by the Nordic gods.

ANGELL: Tell us quickly.

LEIF: A case of bottles. Because it floated we knew that it must contain something aerated, and, sure enough, there were twelve bottles of beer. We have consumed half; the other half we have in this sack, along with some food—which we will not offer you because it may be contaminated.

ANGELL: Our cans appear to be all right, and we will contribute some of those in exchange for the beer.

LEIF: Let us remove this unpleasant object from the scene of our festivity. *To Eric:* Farið með líkið.

*Eric takes the gangster's body by the feet and drags it offstage left. The others sit down on the pavement, the two groups a few feet apart. They exchange the cans of food for the bottles of beer and proceed to open them up and prepare a feast. The two families sit facing each other.*

LEIF: This festive occasion, my friends, marks the fortunate ending of two long and perilous voyages. What is that red feather which the lovely maiden wears in her hair?

ANGELL: That is supposed to be a magic charm of the Vichadas; it keeps the demons and evil spirits away.

LEIF: The demons have already been here, and they are dead. The evil spirits, I hope, will not follow us as we sail up the Hudson River. The feather reminded me of the search for Freyja, our Nordic goddess of youth and beauty. In one of our lays, "Edda of Saemund the Learned," she is asked:

> Wilt thou me, Freyja,
> thy feather-garment lend?
> Bind thee, Freyja,
> in bridal raiment.

Will you play the part of Freyja at our feast, Myrna?

MYRNA: Alas, the only raiment I have is an old grass cloak that is falling to pieces.

LEIF: You yourself are intact, and that suffices. In our poem the goddess disappears, and the unhappy lover laments:

> Treasures have I many,
> necklaces many;
> Freyja alone
> seems to me wanting.

ANGELL: As we sail up the Hudson River we shall come to the Washington Irving country, with its legends of Sleepy Hollow, and Rip Van Winkle, and the Headless Horseman, and the little old men who made the thunder by playing at bowls. On the long winter nights we may beguile our fancy with these legends, along with those of your forefathers in the Northland.

LEIF: I will tell you the story of Thor, the god who made our thunder, and of his hammer which was stolen. Thor set out to find the thief, and Freyja went with him, posing as his bride. They sat down to a feast much more bountiful than our own, I am sure. This too is from the "Edda of Saemund the Learned." The hosts were astounded by the tremendous appetites of these gods. The hosts commented:

> Thor alone an ox devoured,
> salmons eight
> and all the sweetmeats
> women should have.

> Where hast thou seen brides
> eat more voraciously?
> I never saw brides
> feed more amply,
> nor a maiden
> drink more mead.

Let us open our bottles. *They do so; he raises his bottle high, and they follow suit.* Here is a miracle; Arctic and the Equator have met; and out of this meeting will come a new race dedicated to peace, brotherhood, and mutual aid. I give you the Icelandic drinking word: Skál!

*They all echo the cry and drink. They have just got settled to eating when a hissing sound from the sky begins to be heard.*

BOB, *gazing up:* Look! Look! There's something in the sky.

*The others turn to gaze; some rise. The sound grows continuously louder.*

LEIF: Some kind of huge rocket device; you can see that it is driven by jets.

ANGELL: It is being slowed by reverse jets. It is coming straight at us.

BOB: No, it is turning.

*All this time the sound is growing louder. They rise and stare with increasing excitement.*

LEIF: Apparently it is going away again.

ANGELL: It is being turned by jets in the side; a most ingenious device.

BOB: It's stopping. It's going to let itself down backwards. Get out of the way.

ANGELL, *pointing left:* No, it is planning to land out in the drive. *He has to shout to be heard above the hissing roar.*

LEIF: I never saw anything to equal that. They have turned completely upside down and are letting themselves down gently.

ANGELL: It is a spaceship. They may have come from another planet.

BOB: Look! They are putting out braces at the sides to hold it up. They are going to land.

LEIF: A most skillful performance indeed!

ANGELL: We do not know what may come out of this vessel. They may be dangerous. Here, take this. *He hands the pistol to Leif, then picks up the tommygun and holds it in readiness.*

LEIF: Is there going to be more killing?

ANGELL: We must be prepared to defend our women.

Bob: They have landed; we shall soon know.

*The sounds have died away.*

Leif: Certainly these are civilized beings, whoever they are. That maneuver was a marvel of technical skill.

Angell: I believe I know who they are; I have seen pictures of this apparatus. It is Hastem. Surely there can be but one like it.

Leif: What is it—this Hastem?

Angell: The Harry S Truman Expedition to Mars. It set out while I was living on the Orinoco River, before we fled to the jungle. Just a few weeks before the war broke out.

Leif: Oh, I remember! They must have been away for fifteen years.

Bob: See! The doors are open. They are coming out.

Angell: Two men. It's all right, I believe.

Leif: They will surely not be enemies.

*During this episode the two girls have moved each to her lover, and for the rest of the scene they stand, Eric with his arm about Myrna, and Bob with his arm about Elfrida; two love scenes in pantomime.*

Engstrom, *calling off left:* Hello! Who are you?

Leif: We are friends.

ENGSTROM: Then why do you carry guns?

LEIF: We are afraid of you. Who are you?

ENGSTROM: I am Captain Engstrom of Hastem, the Harry S Truman Expedition to Mars.

LEIF: You have been there?

ENGSTROM: For a long time. We could get no signals for our return. What is the matter?

LEIF: Tell him, Doctor.

ANGELL: The matter is there are no people left.

ENGSTROM: No people left? What are you telling me, man?

ANGELL: There was war, and it turned into a biological war, and most of the people have been killed.

ENGSTROM: You mean to tell me that there are no people in New York?

ANGELL: Very few, and most of them are of bad character. You will have to guard yourself against them as we are doing.

ENGSTROM: For God's sake! *His voice has been getting louder as he speaks, and now he strides on. He is a robust man of middle age, in the uniform of an aviator. The other man follows.* I am Captain Engstrom, of Hastem, and this is my pilot Morgan. Who are you people?

LEIF: I and my grandchildren are wanderers from Iceland. My name is Leif. This is Doctor Angell, and his son and daughter.

ANGELL: Botanist of the Rockefeller Institute, sent to the jungles of the Orinoco River, and just recently returned.

ENGSTROM: Well, gentlemen, this is a strange meeting. For fifteen years we have been trying to get signals from America and failing. Now we learn the reason. How long have you been in New York?

ANGELL: Only a few days, and already we have had two encounters with gangsters and have had to kill three men. There is no longer any law. We understand that it is the same out in the country.

ENGSTROM: This is painful news indeed. We have weapons, but we have never had to use them on Mars, and we did not expect to have to use them in our homeland. We must get to Washington and report.

ANGELL: We recently talked to a man who had come from there, walking all the way. There is nobody left in Washington. There is no government, and no chance for you to report.

ENGSTROM: We feared some trouble, but this seems beyond belief.

ANGELL: Apparently we used on the enemy the same weapon he used on us, and it worked in both cases.

ENGSTROM: Then the whole earth is depopulated?

ANGELL: We left people in the jungles of the Vichada River in eastern Colombia, but we have seen very few since then. Apparently the Bio, as they call it, has affected all who were in contact with civilization.

LEIF: You have to make your report to us, Captain Engstrom. You have actually been to Mars?

ENGSTROM: We have lived there all this time.

LEIF: What did you find?

ENGSTROM: We found the ruins of a civilization; great cities and temples. They may be thousands of years old, they may be hundreds of thousands of years old.

ANGELL: And no living beings?

ENGSTROM: The whole planet is inhabited by creatures —we do not know whether to call them men. They had tunneled deep underground and learned to live there. We could not find out anything about their ways of living because they closed the holes behind them, and we dared not try to follow. From the signs and sounds we judged there must be enormous numbers of them; we saw traces of their entrances and exits wherever we wandered on the planet.

ANGELL: You were not able to talk to them?

ENGSTROM: We felt a strange kind of vibration which we are sure was their means of communication, both among themselves and with us; but we were not able to interpret the pulses.

ANGELL: You heard them by ear?

ENGSTROM: No, we heard them internally, strange as it may seem. It was kind of an internal quivering, and continually interrupted by dots and dashes.

ANGELL: A kind of intestinal Morse code, so to speak.

ENGSTROM: Exactly so.

ANGELL: But the people never came near you?

ENGSTROM: We decided that they must consider us gods. We came from heaven—from the sky up above them. They were afraid of us and presumably wished to propitiate us. They brought food and left it every night for us.

ANGELL: What sort of food?

ENGSTROM: Little brown pellets, served on deftly made earthen trays. We were afraid of it, thinking it might be poison, so we did not touch it. Then they sent up two of their women, who offered us the food and ate some of it in our presence. We found that it had an agreeable taste and was nourishing. We lived on it all the time we were there, saving our own food.

ANGELL: A most extraordinary thing! How can it be possible for them to produce food under the earth?

ENGSTROM: It must be one of the secrets they have learned through the ages. No doubt they had wars, just as we have, and escaped destruction by going underground.

LEIF: An extraordinary story you tell us, Captain Engstrom.

ENGSTROM: That we knew, and prepared ourselves accordingly. We brought the two women with us.

ANGELL, *in amazement:* You mean that you have two Martian women aboard that rocket ship?

ENGSTROM: I mean just that, sir. They came willingly, for they have become our wives.

ANGELL: More marvels yet!

ENGSTROM: They made it clear that they expected to become our wives, and we were afraid to refuse their offer because we had learned on earth that women do not take kindly to such a rebuff. We were afraid we might make enemies out of those innumerable creatures underneath the surface, and they might find ways to destroy us.

ANGELL: What was the result of this strange marriage?

ENGSTROM: The result was many children. The Martians are extremely fertile, we learned. The birth occurs in a couple of months, and nearly always triplets. The children reach maturity in a couple of years.

ANGELL: What was the nature of these children?

ENGSTROM: Apparently the Martian genes were dominant; they bore no trace of their fathers. They are born with an extraordinary digging apparatus, which hardens in about three hours after birth. They do not suckle, but go right to work to get underground. Some instinct guides them to their fellows; or perhaps they are able to make their own food. We could never find out, for we had no way to ask questions of their mothers.

LEIF: This tale grows stranger and stranger. Could you not learn to communicate with them in fifteen years?

ENGSTROM: We were able to teach them a few words by tapping signals; but we were never able to understand their code, nor discover how their sounds are made.

ANGELL: Would it be permissible for us to see these Martian ladies?

ENGSTROM: We brought them for that purpose. Morgan, will you lead them out?

MORGAN: Yes, sir. *He goes off left.*

ENGSTROM: You understand, gentlemen, you will not find them prepossessing according to our standards. They are rather short. Because of their color we call them the Gold Dust Twins. They have, as you will see, quite wonderful heads. We have been exasperated by our inability to find out what goes on inside them.

LEIF: The thought is truly fascinating!

ANGELL: Imagine the excitement your arrival would have caused if Riverside Drive had been populated by its usual Sunday afternoon crowds and the newspaper reporters and radio commentators had got word of your arrival!

ENGSTROM: We thought of such things, but we became more and more alarmed because we were unable to get replies to our prearranged signals. As we approached the earth it should have been possible to get radio signals—but apparently there is no radio.

ANGELL: We have not been able to make sure because we have no apparatus, and no electricity.

BOB, *gazing off left:* Here come the ladies!

*All turn and stare.*

LEIF: How incredible! I trust that you will not be offended by our astonishment, Captain Engstrom.

ENGSTROM: We have been through all that ourselves, and were prepared for the world's reaction. You must understand, we have become fond of them, for they have proved themselves good and obedient creatures. They dig their way down into the earth, and come up again with cheerfulness, and bring us the means of life.

ANGELL: The most extraordinary spectacle that ever met a scientist's eyes!

MYRNA: Oh, they are perfectly awful!

BOB: I think they're cute. Their heads are the same color as your hair.

*Morgan enters, leading the two Martian ladies. They
are creatures about three feet high, in masks, with coats
made to resemble skin with large silver scales like fish.
Their heads are immensely large and bulbous, with
scalps of bright powdery golden color; no hair. Their
eyes are large and protruding, and each eye turns
separately from the other. Their mouths are small and
recessive. Their bellies are rotund. In place of hands
and feet they have large objects of shiny steel, like
digging claws.*

ANGELL: Here truly is something new under the sun!
If circumstances permitted, I could think of nothing
more fascinating than to study these creatures and try
to solve the mysteries of their being.

LEIF: What do you plan to do with them, Captain
Engstrom?

ENGSTROM: Indeed I do not know. If I had foreseen this
situation I would not have brought them.

LEIF: Do you think they are adapted to survive in our
climate?

ENGSTROM: I cannot imagine why not. If they dig deep
enough they will be below the frost line, and they do
not need to come up for anything.

ANGELL: It occurs to me that it might be a fascinating
experiment to turn them loose. What would they do?

ENGSTROM: I have not the slightest doubt about that;
they will make for the nearest ground and dig. I can

see no harm in turning them loose. People of our sort have proved themselves unable to survive upon the surface of the earth, and it would seem that a subterranean people are called for. They will have offspring.

LEIF, *excitedly:* Ho, ho, ho! The new population for the atomic age! I dare you to try it, Captain!

ENGSTROM: I have never yet refused a dare. Turn them loose, Morgan, and let these people see.

MORGAN, *obeying:* As you say, Cap.

*The two Martian ladies look in every direction with their large eyes, which are moved by the children inside. Their eyes turn to the ground and find the two earthy places in the pavement. They immediately dart to these places, fall on their hands and knees, and start digging with furious speed at the earth, which is soft. They toss it out in quantities and dig their way in. The holes are barely big enough to admit their bodies, and are completely dark so that audience is not able to see inside them. They just see the two Martian ladies dive in headfirst.*

LEIF: By God, they are gone! By God!

ENGSTROM: They will thrive under this good soil of Riverside Drive.

ANGELL: They won't do so well when they get under the pavements of the city, I fear. The buildings all go down to bedrock.

ENGSTROM: Unless I'm greatly mistaken, they will soon find their way under the sand of the Hudson River and into the soil of Jersey. They are pregnant, and it will not be many decades before they have spread under the North American continent.

LEIF: And to Asia perhaps?

ENGSTROM: Sooner or later some of them will be floating on a log across Bering Strait; or someone will take them in a boat and turn them loose on the other side, perhaps as a joke—or perhaps with the idea of enslaving them. A thousand years, ten thousand years, what does it matter? Sooner or later they will possess all the five continents of the earth and all the islands. Nature has equipped them to survive under hard conditions.

LEIF: Nature's fecundity is blind, but it is infinite. We have provided earth with a new population. Too bad we cannot betake ourselves to Mars and confer the blessings of our own civilization upon it.

ENGSTROM: You can if you wish, sir.

LEIF: You mean that?

ENGSTROM: We took along a great supply of fuel, not knowing how much we would need, or how long we would stay. We have used little more than half of what we carried. So we can go, but I fear we would not have enough to come back.

LEIF, *addressing the other members of his party:* My friends, here is a great decision—greater than that of Caesar at the Rubicon, or of Columbus in his little caravel. Shall we seek another world?

ANGELL: I must say the idea appeals to me. I have been unhappy at the thought of gangsters popping up from behind any building and demanding my daughter at the point of a machine gun. The next one might do his shooting first and his talking afterward.

LEIF: It is a far from alluring prospect.

ANGELL: We are assured that it will be no better in the country; in fact it may be worse—there may be more people hiding there. Machine guns without morals present a new aspect of life. Consider, Captain Engstrom, that at any moment one of these lawless men may take the notion that you might have a bottle of whisky in your spaceship. He would shoot you down from ambush in order to get it.

ENGSTROM: If I had foreseen such things I would surely have stayed on Mars.

ANGELL: Tell us more about life there. You have water?

ENGSTROM: Professor Percival Lowell was right in his idea about the canals. They were made to carry water. There are small lakes, and it would be easy to grow crops.

ANGELL: They do not have freezing?

ENGSTROM: We landed near the equator and did not experience any frost.

ANGELL: I have two boxes of seeds that I brought from South America. They are carefully labeled according to their uses—food, medicine, or what not. We can plant them, and what we grow will not belong to gangsters.

LEIF: Tell us, Captain—could you manage to find the locality on Mars to which you went before?

ENGSTROM: We have excellent areographic maps. The location is by the Sabaean Sinus, near the head of the Forked Bay.

LEIF: How far do you call it?

ENGSTROM: About forty-two million miles at present.

LEIF: And how long will it take you?

ENGSTROM: About two weeks.

LEIF: Would you have room for the six of us?

ENGSTROM: It will be crowded, but from what I observe of these young people they would not object to that.

ANGELL: What do you say, Bob? Shall we go and be Martian gods?

BOB: I will go anywhere if I can take my goddess along.

ANGELL: And what do you say, Myrna?

MYRNA: I say the same thing, provided I can have this Northland god with me.

LEIF: Eric, viltu koma til Mars?

ERIC: Ég kem Myrna.

LEIF: He says that he will follow Myrna. Og þú, El-frida, hvað segir þú?

ELFRIDA: Ég segi hið sama, ég vil Bob.

LEIF: She says that she wants Bob. So, Captain, will you take us as passengers? We are loyal people and will do what we can to repay you in services.

ENGSTROM: I want no pay—only friendship and mutual aid. I think this world has made a sorry mess of itself, and I am willing to leave it to the Martians forever.

ANGELL: As for me, with my seeds I can be happy any-where. It will be an opportunity to try new soils.

LEIF: Let us go, and without delay. I do not relish the idea of having to kill any more human beings.

ANGELL: Take this light machine gun, Captain, and mount guard over your precious rocket ship. If your friend will come and help us, we will go down to the boats and get such belongings as we need.

LEIF, *solemnly:* My friends, for ages there has been only one way of leaving this earth, and that way was pain-ful. Men have always felt it proper to accompany it by solemn ceremony. Now we have another way of leaving—more pleasant, let us hope. The occasion calls for a celebration. My grandchildren and I will sing you an old Icelandic song called "Bravely Sails My Bark." It tells the sorrows of parting from what one has loved.

LEIF, ERIC, *and* ELFRIDA *sing:*

> Eikur sá ég að tvær saman stóðu,
> önnur græn, og var með blómi góðu,
> hin var eikin föl og fá
> furðu visin lauf þar á,
> ég soddan sá
> laufeikina leist mér fyrst að reyna,
> lundur stáls nam greina.

CURTAIN

Note: Music and translation may be found in Granville Bantok (Ed.): *100 Folk Songs of All Nations,* published by Oliver Ditson, Boston, c. 1911.